DEPARTURE TIME

Departure Time

Truus Matti

TRANSLATION BY
Nancy Forest-Flier

namelos
South Hampton, New Hampshire

Publication has been made possible with financial support
from the Dutch Foundation for Literature

DEPARTURE TIME

You could already smell the rain. The girl closed her eyes and took a deep breath.

The wind drove red sand across the bare plain and chased it up the hill. Once it got to the top, it swirled around her and teasingly pulled her hair. One strand kept blowing in her eyes. She tried to catch it behind her ear, but it was just a little too short and kept coming loose.

The clouds flew past as if they were trying to outrun one another. In their rush to get ahead, they shut out every patch of blue sky, jamming themselves into a gigantic blanket, gray as lead.

The darker it got, the colder the wind blew around her. The sand struck her bare ankles so hard that it stung. A drop tapped her bare arm. She shivered. Better find a place to hide than to hang around here. A big storm was coming by the looks of things. But where should she go?

She turned in a slow circle, her eyes scouring the plain. All she could see was red earth, as fine as sand. Nothing else. Not anything that looked familiar. She had no idea from which direction she had come.

Her eyes began to water from the strain of staring. Come to think of it, she couldn't even remember how she had gotten here in the first place.

Nervously, her feet kept making the same small circle, around and around. Her bag hung diagonally across her chest and cut into her shoulder. She tried to shift it a little, but it was so heavy that it slid right back. What on earth was in it? No sooner had she squeezed her head under the strap to see what was inside than the clouds burst apart. *Run for it!* She swung her bag over her shoulder and took off, not knowing where she was going. All around her, the drops beat dark, little pits into the red earth. She stumbled down the hill, leaning into the wind. Soon the rain began falling so hard that she could only see a few feet in front of her. Her shorts stuck to her thighs. She thought about her red raincoat hanging on the rack at home. Each time the bag slid from her shoulder, she pushed it back impatiently.

When she finally got to the foot of the hill, something flashed through the sky. Lightning! She huddled down and waited for the boom, but it didn't come. Cautiously, she opened her eyes. Just ahead of her, suspended high in the dark sky, was a bright pink light. After a few seconds, the light went out, and then almost instantly another flashed on beside it. The lights looked like letters. She stood up for a minute so she could see them better. An H ... an O ... a T ... an E ... *Hotel!*

As soon as each of the five letters had taken turns blinking, they all flashed on together, lighting up the roof on which they were mounted and the outline of the building below. Without losing sight of the lights, she hurried on. Suddenly, the O started to flicker. It wavered once more, then went out. Right away the same thing happened to the T. The other letters just continued blinking. First one by one, H ... then nothing, E ... and then the L blinked—twice—all of them in poisonous pink: H, E, L, and L. It only lasted a second, and then all five went on again.

Warily, she made her way toward the building. It was

almost completely dark inside, except for a dim light coming from a small ground-floor window. She tried to peer in, but the glass was all steamed up. All she could see were a couple of shadows.

Next to the window was a narrow door, hanging so crooked that it didn't shut properly. Above it, a sign was swinging back and forth in the wind, its paint chipped off in places. WAI ING R M, she managed to make out. Several feet farther, at the corner of the building, was a bus. It kept appearing and disappearing in the pink flutter of the neon letters.

The wind whistled around the building and pushed her forward. She held out one of her hands to keep from falling. The door swung open, and before she knew it, she had stumbled in. But she stopped short in the doorway, frozen with shock.

A wall of damp warmth slapped her in the face. Inside the air was heavy with the smell of wet dog's fur. Two small stoves on facing walls heated the room. Dirty glasses and plates were scattered across several square tables and cluttering the floor. Some were still intact, but most were broken.

Only then did she see a long, low bar opposite the door. A gray fox was slouched over the tap, his head resting on his paws. The fox's head was slightly cocked so he seemed to be grinning.

Sitting on a bar stool with his back to her was a fat white rat. His bare tail hung down limply, its tip lying in a pool on the floor. He was slumped over with his head resting on the bar. In the brief silence between two gusts of wind, she thought she heard him quietly snoring.

Very cautiously, the girl took a step forward.

"Is anybody here?" she asked. It came out like a sort of whisper.

Nothing happened.

"Can somebody help me?" she said, a little louder now. "I think I'm lost."

Again no reaction. She looked around. Who was she talking to anyway? She took a deep breath so she could be heard above the howling of the wind.

"I'm looking for shelter!" At that very moment, the wind died down. In the sudden silence, it sounded as if she were screaming.

The snoring stopped. One of the rat's eyes shot open and stared at her. She shut her own eyes in terror. When she dared to open them again, the eye was still staring.

Sighing deeply, the fox straightened himself up. He threw back his head and made an elaborate yawn that ended with a little peep. Then he detached himself from the bar and he leisurely shuffled toward her. She held her breath. He was almost as tall as she was!

When he got to within a few inches of her, he stopped and stuck out his paw. She jumped aside anxiously, but the fox simply reached past her and slammed the door with a flourish. Was she seeing things? Was that a wink? She stared at him in bewilderment.

Without taking his eyes off her, he grabbed a chair from a nearby table and slid it back, executing a movement that most closely resembled a little bow.

"Sit down," said the fox. "Make yourself comfortable." His voice was soft and very low. He spoke with difficulty, as if these were the first words he'd uttered in a long time.

"You've come to just the right place."

Forget everything. I figured that was probably the best idea.

Just don't think about anything anymore. Forget what happened to Sky. Forget how stupid I'd been. And if I did forget everything, I wouldn't have to tell Robin, either. Actually, even if I had told her, she probably would have looked straight through me with that glassy stare, nodding slowly, with the same vague look on her face. That's all my mother ever did after the accident: stare past the moving boxes out into space. Every time I came home from school, she'd be sitting just where she was when I left, as if she'd never moved in all that time.

Forgetting had really started to work. I got better and better at it. Robin and I each went our separate ways. We never mentioned the important stuff, which mainly meant we never mentioned Sky. Sometimes it almost felt as if my father had just gone away on the boat, the way he always did. As if he could show up anytime, slipping in a home visit between trips. I got so good at forgetting that I started to believe it myself.

But something's changed in the last few weeks. It happened so slowly that I almost didn't notice it. It started with an empty moving box in the hallway. Then another and another—every day a few more. When I come home from school, I don't find Robin sitting in her usual spot quite so often. And when I say hello, she actually looks at me instead of through me.

Suddenly, before the last box has been emptied, she announces she's going on a trip. To the boat, to settle Sky's affairs.

"Do you have to do that *now*?" I ask, thunderstruck.

"I've already put it off much too long," she replies. "It's about time things started changing around here."

"But why now?" I ask again. "Now that summer vacation is starting and everybody's gone? Now that it's almost my birthday?"

Now that it's all almost a year behind us, I say to myself. *Now that I've gotten so good at forgetting.*

"It won't take long at all," says Robin. "I'll be back before you know it. And certainly before your birthday."

For a split second, I'm on the verge of telling her everything. But at the last minute, I don't. Not now, when she's finally starting to get back to normal. And anyway, how would I explain why I had kept my mouth shut all this time?

The only one I'd dare tell is Sky. I could always tell him anything. My father wasn't an easy person to shock. But he's not here anymore. And if he were here, there wouldn't be anything to tell him. That's the weird thing: If he were here, there wouldn't have been an accident.

You make everything much too complicated, Sky would say if he could hear me now. *You could make a horse go cross-eyed.* And he'd laugh and give my ear a tug. Or muss up my hair. And then he'd stretch out on his back on my bed and hum a little tune.

That was the tough part about forgetting: I had to try so hard not to think about Sky. I don't think I could have kept it up much longer.

Besides, I've got a memory like a steel trap.

"If I were you," said a voice so soft that at first she wasn't sure she'd actually heard it, "I'd make myself scarce."

Startled, the girl turned around. Right behind her was the rat. From where she was sitting, she had to look up at him.

"There's no room here for a girl like you." The rat bent over her. Up close like this, his fur was more yellow than white, with grubby spots.

A girl like her? She suddenly started trembling despite the stuffy warmth. Her eyes searched in vain for the fox. He had disappeared through a pair of swinging doors behind the bar just a minute before.

"Or were you hoping to start that whole song and dance all over again?" The rat fixed his gaze on her, his beady red eyes smoldering. There was a strong smell about him. That smell—she knew it from somewhere.

"Well, I'm not falling for that again." His voice was rising to a shriek. "And speaking of childish, who's being childish now? Ffff!" He spit out his last comment with fury. His breath blew past her ear. She didn't dare move. "I'll give you ten seconds ..."

"I'll give *you* ten seconds to get back to your stool," said the fox, who popped up out of nowhere behind the rat and grabbed him by the scruff of the neck. "Or out you go. That's no way to treat my guests." The fox leaned so far forward that he and the rat came snout to snout. They were exactly the same size. The rat narrowed his eyes to slits and laid his ears down flat. Not a hair on him moved. The fox's gray tail lashed back and forth. Then, as abruptly as he had laid hold of the rat, he let him go.

The rat rubbed a paw over his neck. His mouth opened and shut a couple of times, but no words came out. He slowly backed up a few steps, then turned around and silently returned to his stool.

The girl let out a deep breath. Only now could she feel how hard her heart was pounding. Startled as she was, she watched the rat with curiosity. His tail swept heavily across the floor behind him.

"It seems the rat has confused you with someone else." The fox placed a pitcher of water and a glass in front of her. "Don't pay any attention to him. He'll get over it." He stood watching as she gulped down the water.

The hand holding the glass was covered with spots. She put her two hands together to compare them. The same spots. She picked at them inquisitively with one finger. It looked like paint. In the dim light, it was hard to tell what color it was. Dark yellow, or maybe orange.

"We don't get very many guests these days," said the fox. He gathered a couple of glasses from the floor and stacked them up.

"To be honest, we're both rather surprised." The last word escaped from his mouth like a sigh. Then, with eyes as big as saucers, he turned to survey the rest of the room as if he were seeing the mess for the first time. Zigzagging between the tables, he collected more and more glasses until the stack had grown dangerously high. When he got to the bar, he filled a basin with water and began to rinse them one by one. The splashing of the water and the tinkling of the glasses made the girl feel much calmer.

From the corner of her eye, she watched the rat, who sat motionless on his stool, staring at the fox. Her gaze ran down the length of his bare tail. At about the halfway point, there was a strange kink in it, as if the tail had gotten caught somewhere. She couldn't stop looking at it. There was something about that tail that almost reminded her of something else.

She looked around uncertainly. The rat had acted as if he knew her. If she had been here before, wouldn't she know it? She squeezed her eyes shut and tried to concentrate. All she could remember was how she had come here from that bare hill. Everything else was a total blank.

Maybe she just had to think harder. If only she had the beginnings of a memory, surely the rest would follow. She fixed her gaze stubbornly on the pink tail. But no matter how hard she tried, nothing would come. She didn't have the slightest idea how she had ended up on that hill or why she had come here. She stared at her hands. She didn't know how that paint had gotten on her fingers, either. I don't even know what my name is, she realized with a shock, slapping a hand over her mouth.

"Stop and think, will you!" The rat had half-straightened himself and was screaming at the fox. "You're just letting yourself be taken in!" His voice broke into a high-pitched peep that sent new shivers down her spine.

The fox picked up a tea towel and started drying the glasses. He answered in a tone that was quiet but insistent. The girl listened with concentration. " ... a certain resemblance, no doubt about it ..." was all she could pick up.

"Or are you two in on this together?" The rat grabbed the tea towel and gave it a snap. "That's all we need!" He jumped down from his stool and reached the door in a couple of strides. It wasn't the same door she had used to come in.

"No one here is going to insult me anymore!" He lifted up his tail and looked from the girl to the fox. "No one!" he shouted again, pushing open the door and slamming it behind him with a loud bang.

Acting as if nothing had happened, the fox picked up his tea towel and started in on the next glass. All at once, the girl realized she was still holding her hand to her mouth. She slowly lowered it. With every gust of wind, the rain pounded against the window. The stoves hissed their one-note tune. Suddenly, she was dog-tired.

She was too tired to think, even too tired to be frightened. She couldn't keep her eyes open. Her head dropped forward of its own accord, and her cheek touched the table. The sounds around her faded further and further into the distance, and the warmth folded over her like a blanket.

"Surprise!" Robin bursts into my room without knocking and stands in the doorway with a big smile on her face. I have to keep getting used to the fact that she's feeling better.

"Mom! I don't just barge into your room, do I?" I peer over the edge of my book, trying to look as severe as possible.

Robin rolls her eyes and dismisses my comment with a casual wave of her hand. In the other hand there's a white bucket, which she is holding up triumphantly.

I lay my open book face down on the arm of the chair and scramble to my feet.

"We're finally going to cheer this place up." The bucket is full of orange paint. "It's about time." She looks around as if she's suddenly noticed how downright bleak it is in here. "We've been living here now ..." Her voice fades away. She puts down the bucket.

Almost a year, I say to myself.

"What do you think of this?" She taps the bucket with her foot. Before I can answer, she goes on.

"You could use a lively color down here in the basement. First we'll paint over that gloomy purple." She puts her palms on the wall as if she were trying to push it away, color and all.

"How on earth did we pick out a color like that?" A shadow

flits across her face. She shakes her head and rubs her hands together. Then she smiles again and turns toward the door.

"By the time your birthday comes, your room will be all set. And when we're finished here, I'll start on the living room." As she talks, she climbs the stairs. I follow right behind her, finding this rather hard to believe. Could she have changed her plans?

There are two more buckets of paint in the hallway, right next to the front door. Next to her suitcase.

"What do you think—good idea?"

I nod. Sure it's good. "But ..." My skeptical eyes turn to her suitcase. She notices.

"As soon as I'm back, we'll start." She pushes the buckets into the corner under the coat rack.

What was I thinking? That she had suddenly changed her mind? That my days of moaning and groaning had actually helped, and that she'd decided at the last minute to stay home? Even so, I do feel disappointed.

"Why can't I come?" I ask for the gazillionth time. "Everybody in my class is on vacation except me." I pull on my sneakers without loosening the laces and start searching for my bag among all the jackets.

Robin sighs. "Because I want to settle your father's affairs as fast as I can. The orchestra has been patient with me long enough. They've been helping us for almost a year now, which is great." Again that flash of a shadow.

"There just won't be any time to do fun things together on this trip. My new job starts in a few weeks." She walks over to me and puts her hand on my head.

"I don't want to stay here alone." I duck and angrily push aside the paint buckets. Maybe my bag has fallen on the floor.

"Alone?" Robin chuckles. "Don't let Birdie hear you say that." She stacks one paint can on top of the other. "You usually love it when Grandma comes to babysit."

"Babysit? I'm almost twelve!" My bag is lying on a pile behind the bucket.

"Stay overnight, then."

"And what if you're not home in time for my birthday? What then?"

I tuck my head under the strap and hang it across my chest.

"That's won't happen." I can hear the impatience creep into her voice. "I'll be back well before your birthday. I promise."

"That's what Sky always said!" I'm already sorry, even before blurting out all the words. Robin rubs her eyes. Nervously, I look into her face. Why isn't she saying anything?

Finally, she opens her eyes, throws an arm around me, and pulls me close. My eyes are starting to sting, so I pull away and open the front door. It's muggy outside. The sun has disappeared behind the clouds.

"You won't be gone long, will you?" She points to my bag. "Birdie could show up any minute."

I shrug my shoulders. She knows very well that I always take that bag wherever I go. You never know if you're going to find something valuable along the way.

"I'm going out to meet her," I tell her, walking down the steps.

"That's nice of you." Robin is standing in the doorway and looking up into the sky. "Put on your raincoat. It won't be dry for long." She holds up my red plastic coat.

"That thing? I can't walk around in that." I take the last few steps in a single jump.

"I thought you liked it so much!" She sounds surprised, and a little disappointed.

"That was last year. When it still fit me. Now it just makes me look stupid." I take a left in the direction of the bus station.

"Next time we'll go together!" I hear her call, just before turning the corner.

A bright light shining straight into her eyes rudely interrupted her. *Go away,* the girl wanted to say. *Or you'll wake me up, and I'm having such a nice sleep.* She turned over, all cozy and warm. The mattress bounced slightly as she moved. The light began slinking toward her eyes once again. She folded one arm over her face to shut it out. "Leave me alone," she murmured drowsily. Then something gently tickled her cheek, as if it were sniffing around. She hunched up her shoulders and giggled. *I don't want to dream about tickling,* she said to herself. *I can't stand to be tickled.* The sniffing stopped, but started up again almost immediately. And what was that smell? It was a heavy sort of smell she knew from somewhere else, the smell of—

"Gasoline," she muttered. That was it. Then she remembered where she had smelled it before. She shot straight up with a shriek. It was the smell coming from that rat.

"Take it easy! I won't hurt you," the rat whispered urgently. He was standing next to her bed, holding a flashlight. "Look. It's me." He turned the flashlight around and shone it on himself from under his face. A gigantic shadow appeared on the wall behind him. "Pipe down, before the fox hears you!" he squeaked in a panic, waving his paws frantically in the air so his shadow danced wildly back and forth.

"He said I wasn't supposed to disturb you, but I *had* to take a look to see if it was you or not." He turned the flashlight around again. The light was blinding. "Sure enough. It's not you. That's obvious."

She slapped her hands over her eyes. The rat switched off the flashlight.

"How about turning on a lamp?" she asked. There was a quiver in her voice that she didn't want to be there. She heard the rat rummaging around next to her bed and she cautiously peeked between her fingers. The pink neon light shone in through the balcony doors and lit up the rat's silhouette. She sat up rigidly and waited until a lamp clicked on next to her ear. A small circle of light fell on the bed. The rat put the flashlight on the night table and stared at her intently.

"I see you sitting here, even though I can still hear the same old racket. The only explanation is that it's not you. Whoever *you* are."

Racket? What did he mean? She couldn't hear a thing ... only the sound of muffled music way in the distance, so soft she couldn't tell what instrument it was.

"I should pay more attention." The rat quickly rubbed his ears with his front paws a few times, back to front, and then along his snout to the ends of his whiskers. It was a comical gesture. Almost ... shy. "The fox knew right away. Not who you are, but who you aren't. He has a better nose for things like that."

"Who I'm not? Who *am* I not, anyway?" she asked. *And how did I end up in this bed,* she wondered.

"A real hotel guest ..." The rat sighed deeply. His red eyes gleamed in the soft light. "We've given you the finest room in the hotel." He spread out his paws and dropped back onto the bed. The girl bounced gently with him.

"You fell asleep in the middle of the waiting room," he continued, as if he had been reading her mind. "The fox thought it would be a shame to wake you. He carried you up the stairs." He folded his paws behind his head and looked at her gravely.

"I'm sorry I snapped at you downstairs." He scrambled up and stretched out a paw to her. Cautiously, she laid her hand on top. The pads on the inside of his paw felt rough yet soft. He covered her hand right over with his other paw. It was such a friendly thing to do that it made her smile. Suddenly she hadn't the faintest idea why she had been so afraid of him.

"A real guest!" he repeated. He squeezed her hand, as if he still couldn't believe it. She shut her eyes for a minute and sniffed the gasoline smell. It really wasn't unpleasant at all. There was something about him that felt familiar.

"If I'm not who you thought I was," she suddenly asked, "then who am I?" She blurted it out before she knew what was happening. She didn't dare look him in the eye.

"What are you asking me for?" The rat let go of her hand. His surprised voice shot up even higher.

"Because I don't know myself." She stared at the little bump that her feet made under the blanket. "I've forgotten everything. I don't even know my own name."

"I'm always forgetting stuff." The rat shrugged his shoulders carelessly and jumped off the bed. "Where I put things, or what I wanted to say. And the harder I try to remember, the worse it gets." He tapped her cheek lightly for a moment, one claw scratching gently. Then he clicked off the bedside lamp and turned on the flashlight at the same time. A circular spot of light shone on the floor.

"As I always say, the best way to look for something is not to look for it. The trick is to look right beside it, if you know what I mean." The bundle of light slid across the floor in front of him.

"Then you see what you see, and not what you think you ought to be seeing. And before you know it, you find just what you're looking for. But without *knowing* what you're looking for." The bundle of light had reached the door, lighting up the threshold.

"Sweet dreams." The rat pushed down the door handle. Before she could say another word, he had slipped out through the crack. The door latched quietly behind him. In the silence, she could still hear the music playing very softly.

The sound seemed to be coming from outside. She slipped out of bed and walked to the balcony doors. The handle sprang open with a snap, and the music wafted in with the fresh air, so clear now that she could easily tell it was a piano. The sound seemed to be coming from above.

Behind the balcony doors, there was only an iron rail. She leaned over the rail as far as she could. Everything below her was dark. Apparently, her room was on the second floor. Except for the flashing neon letters, she couldn't see any light above her, either.

The tune she heard was always the same. It went on and on, relentlessly, one tone stumbling over the next. Up a bit and then back down. Then up again ... faster and faster, louder and louder. *As if an angry person were playing,* she said to herself.

Suddenly, she started shivering. Her shorts still weren't completely dry after this afternoon's storm. She hung them over a chair near the foot of the bed. *I have a feeling I've heard this music before,* she thought as she slid trembling between the sheets. She pulled the blanket up to her chin and turned over on her side. Or maybe she was just imagining it because she'd been listening to it for so long.

The piano is playing very softly, but I wake up right away. This can mean only one thing. Sky is home!

I roll out of bed drowsy from sleep and stumble down the hall. Looking through the crack in the living room door, I can see the backs of Sky and Robin. There's just enough room for the two of them on the piano bench. The door squeaks when I push it open. Sky turns around. And before I know it, I'm sailing through the air. The stubble on his chin scratches my cheeks. I have to sneeze hard, twice. Sky laughs and puts me down.

"I brought something for you!" He pushes a package into my hands. I'm still groggy from sleep. And as I fumble with the string wrapped around the package, Sky tears the paper open impatiently. Something red appears. Red and shiny.

"All the way from Italy!" He holds up the raincoat for me as I grope for the armholes with my hands. "It looks great on you!" Sky turns me around a couple of times. His dark eyes gleam from so close up, with his stubble right underneath. Close enough to touch. The plastic of the raincoat smells sweet. It crackles a little when I reach out my arms to him. The ends of the sleeves hang down limp, and my hands are hidden inside.

"It's much too big for her!" Robin's laugh sounds like singing. "She's nine, remember! Not eleven!"

Robin squats down in front of me and rolls the sleeves up one by one. Her nails are the same beautiful, shiny red as my raincoat.

"No, it's not. Just a bit on the roomy side. At her age, she'll grow into it in no time." It's as if the dark voice itself is picking me up under my arms and swinging me around, crackling in the brand-new plastic. Once again, I sail high in the air, around and around, with my head getting lighter and lighter. Each time I pass Robin's laughing face, I try to look into her eyes, but I'm going too fast. I'm getting dizzy. I close my eyes. I have to laugh so hard that I can't hear the crackling anymore. I feel light and heavy at the same time.

Was that the door clicking?

The girl had the distinct feeling that someone had been in her room. Maybe the rat had come back. She held her breath and listened, but there wasn't a sound to be heard. Cautiously, she opened her eyes. Pale morning light came in through the balcony doors. Fresh air brushed her cheeks.

She sat up and looked around, wondering what was going on. Everything in the room was pink. There was pink-flowered wallpaper on the walls. The fabric on the chairs and the curtains repeated the same pattern. It made her dizzy. She slipped out of bed and walked across the pink carpet to the window. The sun was doing its best to drive off the morning mist. Only the top of the hill was still wrapped in fog.

With her eyes, she retraced the route she had taken yesterday. Down the red hill to the plain, the sudden thunderstorm, the animals in the stuffy café that wasn't called a café but something else. What had the rat called it again?

Waiting room ...

That was exactly the right word for this place. "We don't get very many guests these days," the fox had said. It was as if the animals were just sitting around waiting for something but had almost given up hope. Everywhere you looked, you got the impression that nothing ever happened here. With her finger, she rubbed a space clean on the dusty window and stared outside. Less than twenty-four hours ago, she had walked here, in the pouring rain, and—

Hey!

She had been carrying something then. She was sure of it. A bag! How could she have forgotten? A white bag. She remembered how it kept knocking against her leg as she ran. But she didn't have the bag with her when she got to the waiting room. It must have slid off her shoulder during the thunderstorm without her noticing it. She narrowed her eyes and gazed across the bare ground. It must still be lying where she dropped it. Maybe the bag would help jog her memory. She had to start looking for it right away!

She picked up her shorts from the chair where they were hanging, and something fell out of the pocket and onto the carpet. She picked it up. It was a key, an ordinary house key. It was hanging from a silver metal chain. Was this hers? There was a kind of pendant attached to the chain, but she couldn't quite make out what it was. She slipped on her shorts and put the key back in her pocket. Then she stepped into her sandals without loosening the buckles and walked to the door.

The hall was dimly lit. The walls had shoulder-height wood paneling and a row of little lamps, but only a couple of them were working. The stairwell was just opposite the door to her room.

As she went downstairs, the carpeting absorbed the sound of her footsteps. Fortunately, no one was in the lobby. On the far side were two double doors, with sunlight pouring in through little yellow panes.

Walking on tiptoe, she crossed the wooden floor. The floor was full of nicks and dents, and it creaked in places. In the middle was a big circle filled in with little pieces of wood, which looked like an enormous puzzle. The sunlight fell across it in diagonal bands and lit up the dust that danced just above its surface. She slowed down a little out of curiosity but didn't take the time to stop.

The door to the outside opened noiselessly. It was chilly out there. The bus was near the corner of the building, just past the sign. Only now, in the light of day, could she see what bad shape it was in. One of the tires was flat, which made it sag a little to one side. The door had fallen open. The bus was so encrusted with dirt and grime that she couldn't tell what color it was. *Could be brown,* she thought as she hurried past it toward the hill.

Now that she had to climb it, the hill seemed much higher than it did yesterday. As she walked, she carefully studied the surroundings. A white bag in the red dirt—something like that was bound to stand out. Halfway up the hill, she paused to catch her breath. The sun had burned away the last of the fog. It was quickly warming up. Only now did she realize how hungry she was. When was the last time she had eaten anything, anyway? Refusing to give in, she put one foot in front of the other. By the time she reached the top, she was breathless.

The bag was nowhere to be seen. Yet she was sure she had had it with her yesterday. Disappointed, she sank onto a nearby stone and picked absentmindedly at the paint on her fingers, which loosened and fell off in little flakes. Out here in the daylight, she could see the color much better than in the waiting room. The orange showed up brightly in the sun.

Where could her bag have gone so quickly? She put her elbows on her knees and rested her head in her hands. She always thought better that way.

Always? she said to herself with surprise.

"How can I bring you breakfast in bed if you're not even there?" said a low voice right behind her.

She jumped to her feet and turned around. Staring at her with a look of disapproval were the dark eyes of the fox. How did he creep up on me like that, she wondered? Dizzy from standing up so fast, she took a step backward and stumbled over the stone she had been sitting on. Before she could catch her balance, she found herself sprawled on her back in the sand.

"You see? That's just what I mean." His pointed head came into view in the sky above her. "It's all because you haven't had anything to eat." With great care, he helped her up and brushed the dust from her clothes. "Walking in the sun on an empty stomach! And how did you expect to get back? Didn't think of that, did you? Of course not." He looked her over from head to foot, deep in thought. Still a little shaky, she leaned against him for support.

"We'll never get anywhere at this rate." The fox grabbed her arms, turned around, and lifted her onto his back without so much as a by-your-leave. Before she knew what was happening, he had started bounding down the hill. He moved effortlessly, as if her weight made no difference at all. She opened her mouth to protest but soon shut it again. There was no getting around it: This was a great way to travel.

"What could be more urgent than a decent breakfast?" the fox grumbled as he walked. Then all at once he stopped, brought up short by a staggering thought. "You weren't going to leave already, were you?" He almost dropped her. "Now that you've just arrived?"

"I was looking for my bag." The girl tightened her grip. "I lost it yesterday. Because of the thunderstorm."

"Ooh." He sounded almost relieved. "What was in it?"

"I don't know ..." She hesitated. "But I hoped I would find something that could help me figure out what I ... what I'm looking for here. Because I don't know that, either." Suddenly she felt a little silly.

The fox said nothing.

She looked down over his shoulder. The white front of the hotel shone brightly in the sun. From here, it looked like a toy house that someone had forgotten to put away. No wonder she had missed it yesterday in the twilight.

"At least you know you're looking for something," the fox said finally. "That's a good beginning. Even though you don't know what it is yet." It wasn't a question as much as a conclusion he had come to.

"Except for your bag. Because you already know that's missing. So we'll start from there," he added methodically.

The girl listened in amazement. His words made her think of what the rat had said last night. But the way the fox put it, her problem seemed to be getting simpler instead of more difficult. Suddenly she felt much more relaxed. She laid her head against his gray fur and bounced along as he walked. The stiff hairs scratched her cheek.

"What does the bag look like?" the fox asked when they reached the bottom of the hill. With her ear against his fur. his voice sounded even lower than usual.

"White. With a long strap." She let go for a few seconds and stuck her hands out in front of him to demonstrate how long it was. The fox opened one of the doors, bent over a little, and stepped into the lobby.

"Very good. That's clear enough then," he said carelessly, as if he knew exactly where to look.

Sky comes storming into my room with my new raincoat in hand. I'm lying on my bed, reading.

"Quick!" He pulls out the ladder from under my bed and props it against the skylight. Then he climbs up, pushes the window open, and he's outside before you know it.

"Are you coming or what?" He sticks his head back in impatiently, waving the raincoat.

I take a deep breath and carefully climb up the ladder. The higher I go, the more my legs shake. By the time I get my head through the hatch, Sky is peering off into the distance.

"You see how fast that storm is coming?" He points to it and rubs his hands together with excitement. Gingerly, I make my way toward him across the section of flat roof. Not too close to the edge—that makes me dizzy. I'm afraid of heights. But when I'm with Sky, I feel brave. And in the middle, near the chimney, it's not so scary.

I gaze to where he's pointing. The sun is shining overhead, but dark clouds are racing toward us in the distance. Together we watch as a wall of rain comes closer and closer. The raindrops are dazzling in the bright sunlight. Like a silver curtain, the storm bears down on us.

"The devil is beating his wife!" shouts Sky.

"What?!" I have to shout to be heard above the wind.

"That's when it rains and the sun shines at the same time!" He stretches his arms up and grins. I can feel the first drops.

"We're going to christen your new raincoat!" he shouts into the wind. He bows solemnly and holds it up for me. I stick an arm into one sleeve, but I can't find the other armhole.

The rain gradually overtakes the sun. Drops are pounding on the roof all around us.

Finally, my arm finds the other sleeve. I turn around. The rain is hammering down harder and harder. It's pouring from the sky in buckets. We're right in the middle of the storm. All that's left of the sun is a narrow strip on the horizon.

Screaming, we chase each other around the chimney. In no time at all, Sky's light blue T-shirt has turned dark blue; it's plastered to his body. I splash through the puddles in my bare feet. The water feels warm against my legs. I stretch my arms out sideways. The sleeves of my raincoat are so long that I can flap the ends of them up and down like red wings.

Only when the rain starts slowing down, do we climb back in through the hatch, shivering.

After we've both changed into dry clothes, Sky gets his trumpet and sits on the side of my bed. I have to squeeze past him to get to the foot end so I can hang up my wet towel. We call my bedroom the mini-room because it looks more like a closet than a room. My bed only fits in one direction with just enough space for a tiny night table. The ladder to the roof goes under the bed.

"I have to leave a day earlier than I had planned." Sky turns his head and looks at me from the corner of his eyes. "That okay with you?"

I shrug my shoulders. Of course it's not okay with me. But this isn't the first time, and I don't feel like having another quarrel about it. Especially since he has to leave so soon.

"I'd rather stay home longer myself, but I don't have any choice." He doesn't wait for an answer. He puts the trumpet to his lips and starts tooting very softly.

I love this tinny sound. He can make it squawk and howl, but he can make it whisper, too, just like now. The rain is still gently keeping time on the skylight. I snuggle up behind him with one ear pressed against his back. I stick a finger in my other ear so I can hear the music come right through his body.

He's playing scales. You have to do that every day so you don't lose your touch. Halfway through, he switches to a little tune. Every now and then he pauses, then starts up again. I don't want him to go away tomorrow.

"I want to play an instrument, too." It surprises me to hear myself say this. "Then I can go with you. Travel all over the world with you, on the boat, playing music everywhere."

"Good," he barks through his back. "You know what instrument you want to play?"

"Piano," I say. I don't even have to think about it.

"Good choice," he growls. A new tune starts up.

"But who's going to teach me? You're always gone."

The tune shifts back to scales. High ... low ... when he's almost at the bottom he suddenly stops.

"Hey! I have a great idea!" Sky waves his trumpet around.

"Malakoff is retiring pretty soon. The old fiddler can teach you!"

Malakoff lives below us. He's at least seventy and he still plays in Sky's orchestra.

"But he plays violin, doesn't he?" I scramble up and sit next to him on the edge of the bed.

"He plays piano, too. Much better than I do ... I think he'd be glad to teach you. And he'd have company to boot." Sky looks at me with a grin and puts an arm around my shoulder.

"What a couple of smarties!" He holds the trumpet to his lips once more and makes a triumphant blast. *Tataa!* It reverberates so hard against the walls of the mini-room that I have to put my fingers in my ears.

It was nice and cool in the lobby of the hotel. The fox slid the girl off his back next to a table with two deep chairs.

"Breakfast first," he said, rubbing his hands together, and he shoved the table a little closer to the chair she had chosen. Then he disappeared behind a nearby door. In gleaming, graceful letters over the door, it said waiting room. That must be the door the rat had gone through yesterday. Faster than she could think, he was back, carrying a tray that he put down on the table. And on the tray, there was a large steaming bowl.

"I made soup," he said. Almost bashfully, he sat down on the edge of the chair across from her, his tail hanging over the armrest.

A strange fragrance stung her nose. Cautiously, she took a sip. The soup was so salty that she couldn't taste any other ingredient.

"And?" The fox looked at her anxiously. The tip of his tail slowly began to curl. She nodded with her mouth full and tried to smile as she forced down the soup.

"Why isn't there anybody else here?" she asked, to change the subject. It was a question that shocked even her, and the words hung in the air over their heads. She took a deep breath and tried another spoonful.

The fox frowned. He looked from the soup to the girl and back again, lost in thought.

"A little bread to go with that, perhaps? How silly of me not to have thought of it right away."

He jumped up and disappeared once again behind the door.

She put the bowl back on the tray, much relieved, and stood up. Then she strolled over to the wooden circle, stopping at the edge. It was some kind of mosaic made of different kinds of wood cut into all sorts of shapes. When she had walked across that morning, it looked black. She hadn't realized that there were so many shades of brown, from very light to very dark. In the middle was a large, irregular spot made of almost white pieces. No matter how hard she looked at it, all she could see was a formless, seemingly senseless cloud, an enormous puzzle with all the pieces scrambled up. She bent over and felt it with her hand. The pieces were glued down.

"You have to look at it from the other side." The rat was standing by the outside door. He walked to the edge of the circle just opposite her and waved her over. She went, filled with curiosity. He pointed to the middle of the circle and opened his mouth to say something when the fox came back.

"Bread! Freshly baked!" He held up a basket and walked to the little table. There was something white clamped under his other arm.

The rat shot through the lobby and grabbed a piece of bread from the basket. It disappeared in one gulp.

"Hands off! That's for our guest!" shouted the fox. The rat bent over and sniffed the bowl on the table.

"Leave that alone!" The fox made a gesture as if he were brushing away a fly. In a flash, the rat snatched a second piece of bread. And before the fox could catch him, he raced back to the girl.

"The fox likes to pretend he's boss of the hotel so he thinks he can tell everybody what to do," he said with his mouth full. He winked and offered her the other piece of bread. "Be careful. Before you know it, he'll start sticking his nose into your business, too."

She grabbed the bread and took a bite. It was so hard that she had to struggle just to gnaw off a bit of the edge.

"If you would do what you're supposed to do, I wouldn't have to stick my nose into anything," the fox said sharply. "But you'd rather just stand there staring at that wooden goose."

A bird, thought the girl. Now I see it, too. From this side, every piece suddenly fell into place. A big, long-necked white bird was flying right at her with outstretched wings.

"Looks like a swan to me," she said. Suddenly, she felt a shock of recognition. Swan? She stared at the floor in astonishment. What was it about that word?

"My thoughts precisely!" The rat nodded in delight. "Aren't you going to eat that?" he added in a single breath, grabbing the piece of bread from her hand. She watched him absently as he chewed it up and swallowed it with no trouble at all.

"And I suppose this isn't any of my business, either," said the fox. He pulled the white object out from under his arm and held it high in the air.

"Hey!" The rat rushed up to him indignantly. "What were you doing in my workshop? That's off limits to you! Those are my things!"

"Your things?" The fox raised his eyebrows. The rat lunged at the object, but the fox jumped on one of the chairs and barely managed to keep it away from him.

"Give it back!" The rat jumped up and down angrily. "I found that myself!"

"Found it, did you?" The fox raised his eyebrows again. "Ever think about who might have lost it?" He nodded at the girl.

Curious, she came closer. As soon as she saw what the white object was, her heart began to pound. The rat said something else, but she didn't hear him. She let out a cry and stuck out her hands. There was no doubt about it. She'd recognize her own bag anywhere. It was one in a million.

Before I can even ring the bell, Malakoff's door swings open. How does he always do that? Rubbing his hands together, he leads me in. It's stuffy inside. The heater is hissing, even though spring is almost here.

His whole house is full of music books. He had special cabinets built for them. But the cabinets are filled, so the music books are all over the place. In the kitchen, in the hall—there's even a stack in the bathroom.

Malakoff reads music books the way I read regular books. He says that when he looks at the notes he can hear the music. He says music books have stories in them, just like regular books—stories that come to life as you read the notes.

"Time for *quatre mains*!" His eyes sparkle as if he were about to burst out laughing. He has a high-pitched voice that's almost always hoarse and sings a little. You don't expect such a big man to have a voice like that. Yet it suits him.

I slide onto the piano bench. Malakoff pulls up the kitchen chair and sits beside me, thrashing the air above the keys with his fingers. His fingers are just as yellow as the keys.

In the beginning, I was afraid the color of the keys would rub off on my fingers so I was constantly stopping to examine them.

"Why do you keep stopping all the time? Play!" Malakoff

would shout, waving his big hands with irritation. When I finally told him what I was worried about, he had one of his laughing fits that sooner or later turns into a coughing fit, with no end in sight. It's as if he's run out of air.

I've known for a long time now that the keys are yellowed with age and his fingers are yellowed from the cigarettes he's always holding. Sometimes he lights up a new cigarette while there's one still burning in the ashtray—or on the edge of the piano, which is full of little black burn marks.

Malakoff plays the hard part, and I play the easy part. But when we play together, it sounds like a single piece of music. It makes me float, sort of. My fingers fly effortlessly over the keys, as if I were a great pianist.

When we're finished, all I can do is sigh. Playing the piano is great when it's like this. Practicing upstairs all by myself isn't so much fun.

Malakoff looks at me thoughtfully.

"Any mail from Sky recently?"

I shake my head.

"Is he coming home soon?"

"Not yet." My head shakes "no" once again.

"Is it too long for you?"

I shrug my shoulders. It's always long. Malakoff nods silently.

"Here in the city, time seems to pass more slowly than it does on the boat." He gives me a sideways glance. "Waiting takes a long time. Sky just doesn't get it."

We're both quiet for a while.

"Did you know that I thought up that name for him?" he asks suddenly. I look at him with surprise. I didn't know that.

"I've given nicknames to other members of the orchestra

over the years—whether they liked them or not." He winks. "But in Sky's case, the name fit so well that no one ever calls him by his real name anymore."

Malakoff chuckles softly.

"Sky comes from skylark. That's a songbird. When he gets going on that trumpet of his—well, the sky's the limit. I came up with the name because he loves birds so much." Malakoff nods with satisfaction, as if he had come up with the name just now instead of more than ten years ago. "Especially songbirds, of course." He nudges me gently with his elbow.

"I was the one who introduced Robin to Sky when she came on tour to sing. I'll never forget how Sky looked when he heard her name." A new laugh slowly wells up inside him. I hold my breath, but luckily he manages to cut it short. Suddenly, Malakoff slaps me on the leg.

"You know what? How about we start working on something. Something special. And when Sky comes home, we'll perform it for him!" He stands up and starts rummaging through a stack of sheet music.

"Maybe we can try this," he mumbles. He picks up another book and starts leafing through it again. "Or this? It's not easy... ."

Finally, he comes back with a book in each hand.

"Another good thing about time going so slowly here"—he sticks up both arms and waves the books in the air—"at least, we'll get plenty of practice!"

"Music books?" the girl said with surprise. "What am I supposed to do with these?"

She put the little stack of books on her lap and held her bag upside down. The only other thing that fell out was a roll of tape.

"I had no way of knowing that stuff was hers." The rat walked back forth excitedly and gestured to the fox. "Or I would have given it back. Honest!"

The fox stood with his arms crossed and said nothing.

"Nobody ever tells me anything around here." The rat sat down in the chair opposite the girl and started to pout.

"Tell me exactly where you found it," she said insistently.

"Somewhere at the bottom of the hill." The rat made a vague gesture behind him.

"Are you sure everything was still in it?" She leaned forward.

"There wasn't anything else. I searched all around very carefully." The rat was looking at the fox, not the girl. "I unpacked everything when I got inside so the pages would dry out."

She counted the books in her lap. There were nine. They were still quite damp, and the paper had started to pucker. She leafed through a couple of them. They gave off a stale smell of old cigarette smoke. She slammed them shut with disappointment.

"They mean anything to you?" the fox asked quietly.

She shrugged her shoulders and shook her head.

The rat bent forward.

"If you don't do anything with them, may I have them then?" His eyes glistened. "I'm crazy about paper! Gorgeous stuff: You can do anything ..."

"Have you gone completely out of your mind?" The fox went up to the rat and bent over him. "How dare you!" He could hardly get the words out. "Disgraceful!"

"*Now* what did I say?" The rat looked at him in astonishment. "If they don't mean anything to her, wouldn't it be a shame not to make use of such nice material? Now *that's* disgraceful!" He fell back in his chair. "Incidentally, no one has thanked me for finding the bag," he muttered under his breath.

The girl stared at the book on top. Her index finger slid absently across the thick black letters on the cover. b ... a ... c ... h. *If these books aren't of any help to me, the rat can have them as far as I'm concerned,* she said to herself. She put them back in the bag one by one, then threw in the roll of tape. *Don't cry,* she thought, *I do not want to cry.* She held the bag tightly against her chest with two hands.

"Well. There. Happy now?" the fox said reproachfully. "Our first guest in ages is scarcely inside and you manage to bring her to tears."

"I didn't mean to! I ... I ..." The rat looked around, not at all sure what to say. "If you think there should be more stuff in there, I'll help you look for it. Hey—you know what?" He jumped to his feet. "We'll take the bus! I'll drive you anywhere you want to go, and we'll search the whole area!" He placed a paw on her knee for a fleeting moment. "Just say the word and we'll go."

"Don't make me laugh," sneered the fox. "Just how do you

think you're going to get that old rattletrap up and around?"

"Well ... maybe I do have a few problems to straighten out, here and there, but—"

"Problems? A few problems?" The fox switched to a high-pitched squeak and imitated him sarcastically. "It's a wonder it hasn't dropped on its axles already. If I were you, I'd shake a leg and get to work instead of hanging around here and scaring our guest half to death every time you get the chance."

The rat jumped out of his chair.

"And what about you? Have you ever taken a good look at that greasy spoon of yours? Talk about scaring people off. You play the boss left and right—but give the place a little cleaning? Forget it. To say nothing of your so-called food." He gestured angrily at the tray. "No wonder nobody ever comes here. They all go out of their way just to avoid the burned smell."

The girl leaned back in her chair and wiped away her tears. She just wanted them to leave her alone.

"If you don't like the food, you don't have to eat it, do you?" The fox's voice trembled. "Or you could cook it yourself, if you think you can do any better."

"You know what else I don't like? The way you order people around." The voice of the rat grew increasingly shrill. "No one can get anything done around here, with your, your ... meddling!" He hopped from one leg to the other. "Not me, and certainly not her over there."

"*Her over there?* I'm sitting right here, you know. You two act as if I didn't even exist," the girl snapped. The quarrel had really started getting on her nerves.

"You hear that now?" The fox gestured triumphantly in her direction. "Her over there knows perfectly well what she thinks. And another thing—"

"SHUT UP with your screaming! HER OVER THERE can speak for herself, thank you very much. And don't you even know that it's not polite to call someone HER OVER THERE? I'd rather you just called me Mouse!"

The animals looked at her with wide eyes.

She sucked in her breath, amazed at what she had said. It took a minute before it finally got through to her.

No one said a word—until her stomach started to rumble. Then all three of them burst out laughing.

"Nice name." The rat whistled in admiration. "Nice, but small. For a girl like you."

The fox nodded. He rubbed his paws together with satisfaction and grinned broadly. "We'll leave you alone, so you can ... settle in." He patted her on the arm and disappeared into the waiting room. "I've got some urgent business to attend to," he called as he left.

"I've got some work to do, too." The rat dashed to the outside door, pausing in the doorway. A wave of sunlight streamed in.

"Didn't I tell you?" He chuckled softly. "Stop looking for things, and they get found all by themselves." He turned around and walked out. The door closed slowly behind him.

"That was a fantastic performance!" Sky leads the way up the stairs. "And after less than a year! Didn't I tell you that old fiddler was a good teacher?" At the top of the first flight of stairs, he turns around to face me. "I'm so proud of you."

"You think I can learn to play as good as you?" I jump impatiently from one step to the next and back again. Sky is going much too slowly for me.

"Absolutely." Halfway up the second flight of stairs, he stops to catch his breath.

"All these stairs all the time ... the stairs alone are reason enough to move!" He puts his foot on the next step with a sigh. "Climbing like this makes me think of the Stair Climber's Song. If I ever get to the top, I'll play it for you."

After the second flight of stairs, I squeeze past him, run up the third and fourth flights all the way to the top, and open the door. I've got all the lights in the room turned on before he finally comes in. He walks straight to the piano and sits down.

"The Stair Climber's Song! That's not its real name, but it's what I call it." His one hand strikes the piano keys. "The keys go higher and higher, but so gradually that it takes you a while to notice it. You have to really listen to hear it." It sounds a little like a scale. Up and down, up and down.

"I'm no good at trying to play it by heart. All those sharps and flats ..." He shakes his head. "Too bad the sheet music is on the boat. Say, you know what? I'll bring it home for you the next time. Then I'll play it for you as it should be played, with Malakoff."

"Can't you and I play it together?" I tug on his sleeve enthusiastically. Now *that* sounds like fun. Sky cocks his head and looks doubtful. "I have a feeling the score's still a little bit beyond you. You need more piano under your belt."

"Just send me the music," I tell him. "You'll never remember to bring it with you." Maybe I can try to learn it on my own.

Sky nods and jumps to his feet. "In the meantime, we can dance to it." He grabs my hands and pulls me along. "We'll call it the stair climber's waltz!"

There's no trace of a melody in his off-key humming, but that doesn't matter. We waltz together through the living room. Robin has come upstairs, too, and she's leaning against the doorpost, smiling.

Sky lets me go, grabs Robin, and sweeps her away until he trips over his own legs and falls flat out into the blue chair. I drop on top of him.

"The first thing I'm going to get rid of when we move is that crummy old chair." Robin sits across from us and looks at our chair as if she can't wait to get her hands on it.

"No! You can't get rid of this!" I sit bolt upright in a state of shock.

"That thing has *got* to go." Robin looks unrelenting. "It's old and shabby. And faded."

"What difference does that make?" I lay my hand protectively on the armrest. "I want it to stay! I want to keep it!"

The velvet on the corners of the armrests is almost completely worn off. And as far as I know, it's always been more gray than blue. You have to look under the cushion to see that it used to be the color of cornflowers. But I love to sit in that big, old armchair with my hands on the worn spots. Hour after hour. It's the most comfortable place I know. Robin used to read to me there every night. Or Sky, if he was home.

"You're the only one who ever sits in it. I won't have that monster in the living room again. It's only in the way." I can hear from her voice that she's not going to change her mind. I look at Sky imploringly.

"If we find an apartment with a bigger room for you, maybe you can have it in your own room," says Sky. "What do you think?"

"Yes!" I turn to Robin. "Then it won't bother you any-more!"

"There you go encouraging her!" Robin looks at Sky reproachfully. He shrugs his shoulders and grins.

"I give up." She throws her hands in the air and gives in with a laugh. "As long as I don't have to look at it."

Mouse threw her arms in the air and breathed a sigh of relief. Her name slipped down around her like last year's winter coat. It sounded familiar, but it also sounded a little new, because it had been lost.

"Mouse," she said out loud. The word echoed softly through the empty lobby. It made her laugh. Suddenly, she was dying of hunger.

She dipped the tough bread in the soup bowl and listened to the sounds seeping in through the outside door. Something was being dragged across the ground. A few minutes later, she heard water gurgling. Had it started to rain?

She put down the empty soup bowl and stood up. *What was going on out there?* She walked to the door and pushed it open.

"Mouse!" The rat stood near the bus and waved with a garden hose. Water streamed down the sides of the bus. "I had completely forgotten how—how *red* it is!" He shut off the hose and motioned to her enthusiastically.

Without the thick layer of dirt, the bus was unrecognizable. The bright red hurt her eyes. Water lay in puddles all around; here and there, it was still dripping. Sunlight glittered on the windows.

"To think that I let it go so long!" The rat threw down the hose and scurried to the side of the building, where he disappeared behind a door. She could still hear him talking so she walked in after him.

It was dusky inside, and it smelled like wood and oil. She bumped her head on a bare lightbulb that was dangling from the ceiling.

"All that time ..." The rat steadied the bulb and pulled a chain, and the light flickered on. Mouse looked around her, wondering what this was. Opposite the door was a big workbench. There were hammers, screwdrivers, and pliers scattered all over the floor.

"I just never got around to it." The rat walked over to an old armchair in the corner behind the workbench. The upholstery was so faded that you couldn't tell what color it once had been. There was a blanket and a pillow with a flowered pillowcase lying on the chair. Did the rat sleep here?

"How many times have I made up my mind to get started ..." Next to the chair was a big wooden chest. The rat swept a few tools off the lid and began to tug on it. Written in graceful black letters were the words *Outside Light* on the wall where the chest had been. Next to the words was a switch.

"But somehow, something always got in the way." The chest got stuck on the doorstep. Mouse ran to help and started pushing.

"Well, to be honest ... when you get right down to it, nothing got in the way." Suddenly the chest shot over the doorstep and landed with a bang. Side by side, they pushed it through the dirt until it was right in front of the bus.

"And then today, it just happens all by itself. It's downright weird ... as soon as you show up."

The rat wiped his neck with a cloth and shot her a glance. His eyes were gleaming as red as the bus.

"I'll have it running again before you know it." He patted the hood and bent over the chest. "Ha! I knew I must have put them somewhere." He grabbed a pair of pliers and waved them in the air. With one leap, he was in the bus. He opened a latch on the floor of the aisle and dropped to his stomach.

Mouse scrambled behind him up the three steps. Carefully, so as not to tread on his tail, she squeezed past him and walked down the aisle to the back. Everywhere she looked, the plastic on the seats had been patched with bits of fabric in every color of the rainbow. There were even patches that had the same flowers as the sheets upstairs.

"As rusty as anything, those bolts. No wonder, after all this time." The rat cursed quietly and banged on something metal with the pliers.

Mouse dropped onto the rear bench. The seat was getting warm in the sun. The plastic upholstery had a sweet smell. She looked out the window. Bare plain, as far as the eye could see. And how much further after that?

"Is there anything else here besides this bus?" she asked with her nose pressed up against the pane.

"Anything *else*?" The rat stood up and slammed the latch shut. "What could be more beautiful than a bus?" he asked indignantly, pointing all around him with the pliers.

Stunned, Mouse decided not to answer.

"I have a funny feeling the points are rusted," he continued, instantly cheerful, as if he had already forgotten what she had said. "And if that's true, it just might mean ..." But before she could catch the end of his sentence, he was already out of the bus and headed for his workshop.

Mouse watched him go. She lifted her legs from the bench one by one, her bare skin sticking to the plastic. If this bus were the only mode of transportation, it would be a while before she'd be able to leave. She absently picked at the loose edge of a piece of flowery fabric with her finger. As it was, she didn't even know where she was supposed to go anyway.

Looking through the back window, she saw the rat coming out of his workshop with even more stuff, which he began dragging toward the bus.

She sat lengthwise across the bench with her back against the side window and her legs up on the seat. Above the back window was a map.

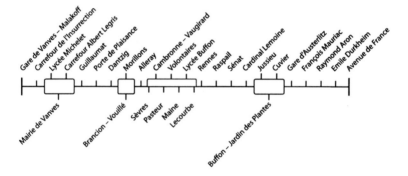

She turned her head to the side so she could read the names of the stops. Lycée, Michelet, Porte de Plaisance ... They sounded like names in another language. She didn't even know how to pronounce some of them. Mairie de Vanves, Cambronne, Vaugirard ... Outside she could hear the rat striking iron with a hammer. As he worked, he shouted something she couldn't understand. Mouse smiled and sank back onto the bench. The hammering stopped. Then he started sawing.

Maybe it wouldn't be so bad to stay here awhile after all. Mouse drew up her legs and nestled down cozily on the rear bench, staring at the map above her head. She wasn't sure why, but here in the bus she almost felt at home.

First a bang, then a quiet shuffle ... Still half asleep, I turn over on my back. *What time is it? Is it light yet? Who's making all that noise?* My eyes don't want to open.

It's quiet again.

But now I can't get back to sleep. It's as if someone has been in my room. I open my eyes a crack. It's still dark. The skylight is open, with the ladder leaning against it.

Suddenly wide awake, I roll out of bed. Fresh air is pouring in through the skylight. Shivering, I grab my raincoat from the hook on the door, pull it on, and climb silently up the ladder.

There are no clouds outside. Spring is here so it's not so cold anymore. Sky is lying on his back on the flat part of the roof, next to the chimney.

"Hey! That raincoat finally fits you." He tosses me a quick glance as I sit down beside him.

"It's a good night for stars." He stares into the sky with his hands folded behind his head. I lie on my back and do the same. The black heavens are bursting with points of light. All I have to do is stick out my hand to touch them. Sky starts humming one of his tunes, the kind of tune that goes on and on forever.

"How are we going to do this after we move?" I ask with a sudden shock of realization. "The new apartment is downstairs.

We won't ever be able to look at the stars anymore." I hadn't thought of that before.

"The new apartment has a backyard. Big enough for a little lawn. We'll lie on our backs in the grass." He looks over at me. "Much more comfortable than this hard roof."

"You won't forget to come and get me then?" I snuggle up closer beside him.

It's as if I can hear him smile.

"That won't be for months!" He puts his arm around my shoulders. "First your birthday. We don't move until then."

Tomorrow Sky has to go away again. After that, it'll be seven more weeks until my birthday. My eleventh birthday ... the last one in this apartment. Just thinking about it makes me sigh. The beautiful new room in the basement of the new apartment is a hundred times better than the mini-room. But never to lie next to Sky on the roof again and look up at the stars? Suddenly I'm not so sure about all this.

"Do you know what you want most of all for your birthday?" he asks.

What I want is for him not to go away, but I can't say that out loud. Whenever I say that it always makes him sigh, and before you know it the mood is spoiled.

"I want ... everything to stay just the way it is right now," I tell him.

"Exactly as it is right now?"

I nod.

Silence for a few minutes.

"So ... no move?"

I shrug my shoulders. That means no beautiful, big room.

"And no birthday!" He teasingly pulls my hair.

"I'll just stay as old as I am now. Ten's a nice number, I think."

"And how about your future as a musician? You play so well."

I have to think for a minute. "Actually, it works out okay," I say after a while. "I'll just keep getting better for my age. Only ten years old, they'll all say, and such a wonderful pianist!"

Sky laughs gently. I shake gently along with him. The piano has suddenly made me think about something else.

"How are we going to get the piano downstairs when we move?" I ask with a troubled voice. That thing weighs a ton.

"The things you worry about!" He laughs again, harder this time, and I shake harder, too. "Everything will be fine." The sound reverberates against the dark sky.

"I think it would be boring," he says after a while, "if everything always stayed the same."

"No, it wouldn't." I look at the points of light above us. "The stars are always the same, right? And they're never boring."

"You think the stars don't change?" Sky shakes his head. "They're so far away that it takes a really long time for the light from one star to get here—so long that a star you're looking at now may not even exist anymore." He stretches himself out. "So what you're seeing now was over and done with a long time ago."

I stare for a minute at one of the points and try to understand what Sky is saying, but it makes me dizzy—and a little sad, too. And I really don't feel like being sad on the last night Sky is home.

Suddenly, I start to shiver.

"You've got to go to bed!" Sky gets up and helps me down the ladder. When we're inside, he turns down my blanket. A book falls on the floor. He has to push two more books aside just to sit on the edge of the bed.

"Books," I say sleepily. "They don't change, either. If you read a book and look at it again later on, it's still the same story. But it's exciting all over again." I say whatever comes into my head, that's how tired I am. Sky's face starts to fade.

"So maybe you should move to an exciting story instead of a new apartment," he says chuckling. He picks up a stuffed animal from the floor. A gray fox. I had stashed it under my bed a long time ago, along with the other stuffed animals. The fox must have come out from under the bed with the ladder. Sky holds him up in front of his face and drops his voice low.

"Ooh! Can I come along? I want to live in a story, too," he growls.

I push away his hand.

"Or do you think you're too big for me? Huh? Now that you're almost eleven, you probably don't even know I exist!"

I give Sky a thump. Sometimes he can be so childish. I grab the stuffed animal and throw it under my bed as far as I can.

"Okay. Then I want a story for my birthday." I have to yawn so hard that I can't talk anymore. I roll over on my side.

"A story?" Sky nods slowly. "I like that idea. But let's make it up together. I'll start." He pulls the blanket up to my chin.

"You have to bring it to me yourself. Then at least I'll know for sure that you'll be home on my birthday." I get tears in my eyes from the yawning.

"Your *eleventh* birthday? You think anybody could keep me away for that? That's the main reason I'm coming home." Sky bends over me and gives me a kiss on the top of the head. "I promise."

Those two words ought to be enough to rouse me. But I want to believe it even more than usual—this time.

Mouse awoke with a start. It was just as if she had heard someone call her name. How long had she been dreaming here, anyway? She was dying of thirst. The rat was hammering on something metal, so hard that each stroke shot right through her.

She scrambled up and pressed her face against the bus window. The sun was sinking slowly behind the hotel. Drowsy from the warmth, she climbed out of the bus, almost stumbling over a spare tire lying at the bottom of the steps.

It was cooler outside. The rat was standing on his toes on a box that had been pushed against the front of the bus, his upper body hidden under the hood. She heard him muttering to himself. Another bang. Mouse chuckled and crossed over to the door of the waiting room, which stood open invitingly. But she stopped short at the doorway. She couldn't believe her eyes.

The room was barely recognizable. The fresh evening air mingled with the fragrance of polishing wax. The floorboards glistened softly. All the chairs were pushed up to the tables. Glasses stood gleaming in rows in the cabinet behind the bar. Above the bar and above each table, little lamps were casting their glow. Suddenly, the swinging door behind the bar flew open and the fox came sailing in.

"Mouse! I was calling you!" He put a big pitcher of water on the bar and was gone in a flash. "The first one is almost ready!" she heard him cry in a muffled voice.

The doors swung gently behind him.

Mouse filled a glass, drank it down, and filled it up again. Only then did she take a seat on the front stool. Halfway through her third glass, the fox reappeared.

"I hope this is better than that soup from this afternoon." With a hesitant gesture, he set a plate in front of her and looked at her apprehensively.

"I still don't really understand why it was so bad."

"Too much salt," Mouse said as she bent forward with curiosity. Now that the worst of her thirst was quenched, she realized how hungry she was. Lying on the plate was a pale, shriveled, steaming crepe.

"Ah! You really think so?" The fox looked up in surprise. "At least that's helpful information."

He nodded cautiously. "The rat never says a word. He gobbles everything down and doesn't taste a thing. If it were up to him, I'd never learn how to cook. Well?" He looked at her expectantly, his head cocked. Mouse gave the crepe a heavy sprinkling of sugar, drew in her breath, and took a bite.

It was still soggy in the middle.

" The first crepes are always duds," she said, and bravely took another bite. "That's normal. And actually, you're supposed to put syrup on them. Have you got any syrup?"

The fox nodded. Then he jumped to his feet with a look of alarm. "My pan!" he shouted as he rushed into the kitchen.

"What did I tell you? Rusty as anything, those points." The rat had come into the waiting room, his fur covered with black grease. He climbed onto a stool beside Mouse and looked with interest at the new plate the fox had brought in.

"This one may be a bit on the dark side," said the fox as he placed the plate in front of her and shoved an earthenware pot next to it.

"Got one of those things for me?" the rat shot out as the fox's back disappeared behind the swinging doors. He watched eagerly as Mouse dipped a spoon in the syrup pot and moved it back and forth over her plate. "What are you doing?"

She turned her plate toward him so he could see what she was doing. But he simply stared back at her with a puzzled look on his face.

"Can't you even read?" She meant it as a joke.

"What's it to you?" the rat asked casually. But he looked so crestfallen that she understood she had guessed correctly.

"I'm writing my name," she said quickly. She had to make the *e* very narrow so it would fit on the plate. "In the hope of never forgetting it again," she muttered under her breath. She rolled up the crepe and took a big bite. The crust was dark and quite hard, but at least *that* meant it was cooked. The fox came back out with the next crepe. She pushed it over to the rat.

"Tomorrow I'm going to try to set them again," he said, reaching for the syrup pot. He dipped the spoon in as far as it would go and held it over his plate. "The points, I mean." He changed his mind and gave the spoon to Mouse.

"Can you write something on mine, too?"

Mouse leaned to the side and started moving the spoon. By the time she had finished the *R* and the *a,* the spoon was almost empty.

"What are you writing?" The rat watched with great attention and sniffed as if he could smell the letters.

"Your name, of course," said Mouse. She didn't have enough syrup to cross the *t* so what it actually said was *Ral.*

"That's not his name at all," said the fox, who cast a cursory glance at the crepe. He shoved Mouse's empty plate to the side and put a new one in its place.

"What do you mean it's not?" the rat asked indignantly.

"You *are* a rat, but that's not your name." The fox put his paws on his hips and looked from the one to the other. "You say 'rat' to every rat."

"But Mouse's name is Mouse?" Puzzled, the rat looked at his plate. The syrup had begun to run.

"Because Mouse isn't a mouse. She's a girl who's called Mouse," said the fox. He nodded as he spoke, as if he had to press his argument home. The rat was silent and stared at Mouse with big, pleading eyes. Mouse, who was just about to write her name on her new crepe, changed her mind and let the syrup run in a straight line, then quickly rolled it up.

"So ... if she were a mouse, she couldn't be called Mouse?" The rat took the spoon from her and dripped an extra spoonful of syrup onto his plate. The fox looked confused and silently scratched behind one ear. To hide his uneasiness, he picked up a soup bowl that was still lying on the bar.

"So what *is* my name, then?" the rat implored.

The fox shrugged his shoulders. "You don't have a name. I don't, either." He stared into the bowl meditatively. "At least not that I know of."

The rat rolled up his crepe just as he had seen Mouse do. He took a big bite. "Then I want one," he said with his mouth full. Resolutely, he took another bite. "Why shouldn't I have a name?" He was surprised at how well he could eat and talk at the same time.

"Where would you get it from?" The fox held up a full soup-spoon and sniffed it.

"How did you get your name?" The rat gestured at Mouse with the rest of his crepe. The syrup ran from both sides and made a trail of drips on the bar.

Mouse shrugged her shoulders. "A name is something you have to get from somebody else." She stuffed the last bit into her mouth and leaned back slightly with a heavy feeling in her stomach.

The rat looked at her thoughtfully.

"I think," he said slowly, "you are exactly the right person to give me a name." He laid a sticky paw on her arm.

"Me?" She pulled her arm away, dumbfounded. "Why me? I've never given anyone a name before. I don't think," she added. Because she wasn't really sure.

The rat bent his head and licked up all the drips of syrup from the bar in a flash. "You did with your own name," he said, polishing his whiskers and tossing her a careless glance. The fox nodded in agreement, she saw to her dismay.

"I only found my name again. I didn't ... invent it," she protested. "I don't think I'm good at making up things."

"I don't want a made-up name, either," the rat said indignantly. "I want a real one."

Mouse looked around uncertainly. She couldn't just pull a name out of the air, could she?

"It has to be something special." The rat jumped from his stool and started pacing back and forth behind her. "Not just any old name that everybody has. You can think it over if you want. Maybe something dignified ... or something foreign ..."

"Foreign?" The word gave her an idea. She looked around toward the open door. Outside, it was getting dark.

"Maybe I do know something." Mouse stood up. "But I need a flashlight. You need a light to find the best names."

The bus to the airport is so crowded that the three of us can't sit together. Robin is somewhere up front, and I'm on the rear bench in the corner, next to Sky. The only place for his backpack is at our feet. I'm sitting with my legs pulled up on the seat.

It's hot in the bus. The sun is pouring in and burning my face. The roof hatch is open to let in some fresh air. I'm tired from having slept so little last night. Every time the bus takes a turn, I get jostled against Sky's arm. I lean my head against his shoulder. The fabric of his jacket scratches my cheek. How can he wear that thing in this heat? I've already taken off my jacket. I close my eyes and sway with the motion of the bus. I hope it takes a really long time before we get to the airport.

"You have to tell me where we're going with this," Sky says after a while. I don't answer him because I'm so nice and cozy, not to mention the fact that I have no idea what he's talking about.

"I don't mind starting, but you have to help me out a little."

He nudges me gently with his elbow. "Or have you already forgotten what we talked about last night?"

The bus takes a sharp turn and swings me to the other side. I open my eyes and pull myself up.

"We were going to make up a story, remember?" Sky raises his eyebrows. "I'll start. Then you pick it up later on."

Oh, yeah! Now I remember. I get right down to business. Now that we're out of the city the bus isn't swaying so much anymore.

"I want ... an exciting story. One of those stories that make you forget everything. Those are the best. It has to be about ... about a girl like me. Not exactly like me, of course. But one who looks like me." I gaze thoughtfully at the back of the seat in front of me.

"Let's say she's lost. Or no—maybe she lost *something*. Something important, but I don't know what it is yet ... and she starts looking for it. She's not just at home, of course. It has to happen in some unknown place. And then ..."

"Whoa! Enough already!" Sky raises his hand. "Looks like you don't need me at all." He smiles at me cheerfully. "Do you know what her name is supposed to be?"

I think a few minutes. That's hard, making up a name just like that. Especially for someone you don't know at all. I shake my head slowly.

"Maybe I've got the answer," he says, winking. "I've got a terrific name in the back of my mind."

I think I know what he's talking about. Before I was born, Sky and Robin each thought up a name for me. In the beginning, they tried out both names. Robin's name won.

"Sounds to me like a good place to start." Sky begins humming a tune.

The bus takes another turn and jostles me against his shoulder again.

"Hmm?" The roaring of the engine makes it hard to hear him.

"A name. That's a good starting place for a story. Especially a beautiful name like this one." He crosses his arms and keeps on humming. "Just the thing for a girl like you."

"Cambronne ... Michelet ... stop me if you hear something you like." Mouse slowly ran the light of the flashlight over the names of the bus stops.

"Hmmm ..." The rat sat beside her on the rear bench with his head thrown back and his eyes closed.

"Carrefour. Guillaumat ... I don't know how to pronounce them exactly. Morillons ..." She gazed up with concentration. "Volontaires, Buffon ... or this: Raspail?"

"Hmmmm ..."

Was he even listening? She turned the flashlight on the rat. He didn't move a muscle. Maybe this wasn't such a good idea after all.

"Sénat? Jussieu? Cuvier?"

Just finding a name was important, too, of course. You shouldn't rush into it. "Buffon? Jar?"

"You already said that." The rat opened one eye. "Buffon. That was one you just said."

The eye closed again. So at least he was listening.

"Jardin, Austerlitz, Mauriac. How about that: Mauriac?" No reaction.

"Aron, Durkheim, Emile ..." She had reached the end of the row.

"What do you think? Any one of those?" Unsure of herself,

she glanced over at the rat. It was darker inside the bus than outside, except for the little circle of light. She saw herself reflected in the window, with the rat beside her.

"How should I know?" He brushed his whiskers without opening his eyes. "You're supposed to pick one."

Mouse sighed. She dragged the beam of light along the row once more, this time from back to front. *It has to be something with an a in it at any rate,* she thought. *That suits him. Raspail? Or was that maybe ... a little too harsh. Too miserly. Mauriac ... . a little too long. Sénat was too short. Not only that but there was an e in it, and that wasn't good. An e,* she thought, *was more for the fox.* She snuck a peek at him. He was sitting on the seat in front of them with his back against the window and one paw along the backrest. Ever since they had gotten into the bus, he hadn't said a word.

She aimed the light further to the left. *Maybe something with a u,* she thought in desperation. *Cuvier?* The light wandered on. Or ...

"Dantzig."

That was it; she knew it for sure. Round at the one end and pointed at the other: just right for the rat. She looked over at him triumphantly. Dantzig sat motionless, his eyes still shut.

"So this is how it feels," he said softly, "when you've found your name."

Everyone was silent. That in itself made it a solemn moment.

"A good choice." It was the fox who eventually broke the silence. Mouse gazed at him thoughtfully.

"Don't you want a name?" she asked.

"Of course he wants a name," Dantzig shouted, before the fox could answer. "This was only the beginning!" He jumped up, as if he had been sitting still way too long, and ran up and down the aisle.

Mouse smiled. *So something with an e for the fox ... Michelet? Legris?*

She mumbled it softly to herself. *No ... there couldn't be an i in it.*

"*Sèvres? Rennes ... hmmm.* The *e*'s were good, and the *r*. But something ... something was missing.

"Well?" Dantzig was so excited, he couldn't sit still. He poked her in the side, making the beam swish back and forth. Mouse lowered the flashlight.

"I can't find it. I'm sorry. There's nothing there for the fox."

"It really doesn't matter." The fox did his best to sound cheerful. "I've done fine so far without one."

"It *does* matter!" Dantzig gave the fox a shake. "You have no idea what a difference it makes." Impatiently, he jerked the flashlight out of Mouse's hands and shined it left and right all through the bus. "It *has* to be here somewhere."

The beam of light shot back and forth. "You see? There are lots more words in here. What's this?" He shined the light on a long sign above the windshield. Mouse came closer. She had to squint to see it well.

IL EST INTERDIT DE CRACHER PAR TERRE. She pronounced it as it was written. *Terre,* she thought. *A little like Rennes ... Two e's, two r's ... it was almost right. And yet ...*

"Maybe my name isn't in the bus," said the fox. He had come up behind them and slid onto the front seat. "Maybe it has to come from somewhere else."

Mouse sat down beside him and stared through the windshield into the dark night. Not being able to find a name for him dampened her happiness about Dantzig. It would be so much nicer to find two names.

Even Dantzig was quiet. He leaned despondently against

the door of the bus and let the light drop. The beam came to rest on the door handle. Mouse's eyes were automatically drawn to the light. She frowned and bent forward. There was something written on the door of the bus. Dantzig followed her gaze.

"You see! I knew there were more words!" He stooped down and poked excitedly in the beam of light with his paw. "What does it say? What does it say?"

Mouse leaned over further. There were two words on the door, in red letters, one on either side of the handle.

OUVRIR was written on the left side.

FERMER was on the right.

"Fermer." She pronounced it as if it were an English word. *That's just what I'm looking for,* she thought with surprise. *It has a good number of e's and r's. And the f at the beginning is nice and sturdy.*

Dantzig nudged her and aimed his light at the fox, who was staring into the darkness with big, glistening eyes.

"It's just as if I always wanted to have that name without knowing it." He looked at Mouse with admiration. "You're good with words," he said.

Mouse felt her cheeks begin to glow. Luckily, it was so dark that no one could see how red she was.

"Party!" shouted Dantzig. "Name party!" He stormed back and forth through the bus until it shook. "Three names in one day! We have got to have a cake!" He grabbed Fermer and pulled him to his feet.

Grinning, Fermer let himself be dragged to the exit. Mouse watched as he hurried toward the hotel with a strange little skip in his step, as if he didn't know how he was supposed to move with his new name.

Dantzig grabbed Mouse by both arms and waltzed her down

the aisle. She tried to keep up with him, giggling all the time, but she got so dizzy from spinning that she soon dropped onto one of the seats. Dantzig danced on alone. To keep away from his frantic spinning, she slid into a corner next to the window.

She saw Fermer in the distance walking toward them. He was carrying something in both hands that eerily lit up his face from underneath. You're good with words, he had said. She didn't really understand why that made her so happy.

"You have to see this as a cake for emergencies." Fermer carefully climbed back inside. "I had a few left over." He put a big plate on the seat next to Mouse. It held a stack of crepes with something sticky smeared all over it. The whole top was studded with candles. There were three candles on the piece Mouse got: a wedge of crepes with syrup in between each layer.

"To think that all this time my very own name had been lying here in my very own bus, waiting for me" —Dantzig grabbed a plate and sat down with it on the seat in front of Mouse— "without my knowing it." He shook his head and absently shoved the whole piece into his mouth all at once.

"Wait till I get this bus running! Then everything's really going to change!" He leaned as far as he could over the seat back and cut himself another piece.

"Everything's changing already," said Fermer. He sat down on the seat next to Mouse and carefully examined his piece of cake from all sides. Mouse chuckled. Did he ever actually eat anything?

As Dantzig talked with his mouth full about a special method for setting the points in the bus, and Fermer inserted a brief question here and there, Mouse took the candles out of her piece of cake one by one and stuck them onto the dish with drops of wax. With her eyes half shut. she stared at the little flames with satisfaction. The voices of Dantzig and Fermer babbled past her.

She yawned and smiled at her reflection in the window. Was it really only yesterday that she had come here? Her eyelids dropped lower and lower. *How come my reflection doesn't smile back,* she wondered sleepily. She opened her eyes and stared at the window. Her reflection stared back angrily. Recoiling in fright, she blinked her eyes a few times and took another look. This time, her reflection looked just as surprised as she did and simply blinked at her. The angry reflection had disappeared.

She held her plate with the candles right next to her head and stared intently at the window. She must have been mistaken. A reflection couldn't have a different expression. And if it did, it wouldn't be a reflection. She was just so tired that her eyes were playing tricks on her.

She pressed her nose against the pane and peered into the darkness. A band of light fell through the door of the waiting room and onto the ground outside. Suddenly, she thought she saw something moving at the edge of the band of light. She stood up and slipped out of the bus.

Outside, it was deathly quiet. The pink light flickered above the empty plain. Nothing moved. She walked once around the bus on her tiptoes. The light from the candles made the animals' shadows dance on the ceiling.

She glanced up at the neon letters. Apparently, the O and the T had gone out altogether. The other three letters flickered on tirelessly. H, E, and then L flickered twice. H, E, L, L ... *No wonder no one ever comes here,* she thought with a chuckle. But at the same time, a shiver ran down her spine. She tried to warm her arms by rubbing them and hurried back to the door of the bus.

"What's the matter?" Fermer was leaning out of the bus, his plate still in his hand.

"For a minute, I thought I saw something outside." She climbed back in past him. "As if something was moving." She pointed behind her, feeling rather sheepish. "But there was ..."

"Nobody. Of course, there was nobody outside." Dantzig jumped up and looked at her innocently. "You must have imagined it." He turned to Fermer. "That's the only explanation."

Fermer said nothing.

"Right?" Dantzig looked at him, waiting for an answer.

"Of course." Fermer took a quick look outside and nodded slowly. "You just imagined it." He touched her arm reassuringly.

"I think we've had enough changes. For one day."

With his paw still on her arm, he bent over the cake and blew out the candles.

The bus station is halfway between our old apartment and the new one. How strange to be thinking about our apartment as "old" while we're still living in it. But that won't be for long. The first moving boxes are ready to go. Day after tomorrow, it'll be my birthday. And after that, we'll really start packing.

The crowds at the bus station calm me down. Robin doesn't think it's a good idea for me to come on my own, but I like it here. I love the smell of gasoline. That's Robin's fault. When she was pregnant, every time she passed a gas station she'd stop a few minutes and sniff the air. Afterward she couldn't understand what there was about it that she had liked so much. With her, it stopped as soon as I was born. With me, it stuck.

There's a wooden hut in the middle of the bus station lot. The buses that are getting ready to leave are in front. Inside the hut, bus drivers drink their coffee while looking out at the waiting passengers.

At the back of the little building is a blank wall. A plank running along the wall serves as a bench. That's where I like to sit, with a view of the incoming buses. I watch the passengers spread out in all directions as soon as they get off the bus. And I try to guess where they come from and what they're going to do. This time, I take an extra good look at their faces, hoping to see Sky pop up among them.

Usually, he lets us know ahead of time when he's arriving. Then Robin and I wait for him together. But we haven't had word yet, which doesn't necessarily mean anything. It's happened before—he gets back before his message reaches us.

The fingers of my right hand drum on the wooden bench beside me. They're playing the melody I've been working on recently, practicing it endlessly until I can play it without any mistakes. I almost know it by heart. I can't wait to see the look on Sky's face when he hears me play it for him.

Here comes another bus. This one's from the airport! There aren't very many passengers getting off this time. It doesn't take long to see that he's not one of them. Even so, I get a little disappointed with every bus that arrives at the station.

I'm really supposed to go home, but I'm going to wait for one more bus before I leave. The next one comes in fifteen minutes.

Where is he, anyway? My fingers drum the wood impatiently.

He promised he'd come especially for my birthday. The words pound through my head to the beat of the drumming: He promised, he promised, he promised.

Someone had made her bed and laid out her pajamas. They were neatly folded and lying on her pillow, waiting for her. Mouse pulled back the covers, grabbed the pajamas, and held them up. Pink flowery fabric. Of course. She chuckled.

There it was again! So soft, she could hardly hear it. She held her breath and listened.

Piano music. Just like the night before. The same melody constantly repeating itself, over and over again. She dropped the pajamas onto the bed and walked over to the window. As soon as she opened the balcony doors, the music grew louder.

With two hands on the edge of the iron rail, she stood there listening. Slowly, the keys crept higher and higher. The fingers of her right hand began to tap along on the railing.

She stared down at her fingers in total amazement. They seemed to know how the music was supposed to be played. Keeping perfect time with the melody, they ran across the iron rail to the right as if they were searching for higher and higher keys. She pulled her hands away from the rail in alarm, shoving them deep into her pockets. *Can I play the piano?* she said to herself with astonishment.

She walked through the room to the door and opened it warily. The music sounded muffled in the hall. It seemed to be coming down the stairwell from above.

She looked all around, not sure of what to do. When Fermer had brought her upstairs just now, he had turned on a big light somewhere. Now the only light came from a small lamp next to the door to her room. The stairs going up disappeared into the darkness. If she wanted to know where the music was coming from, she'd have to go that way.

Carefully, she closed the door to her room and walked across the hall. Her legs trembled as she began to climb. The stairs creaked softly. Each time the piano stopped, she paused and waited till she heard it again.

The third-floor hallway was dark: Not a single light was on. She had to grope her way to the next flight of stairs. As she got used to the darkness, it became easier to climb. This was the right direction. The sound of the piano was slowly growing louder.

Luckily, there was some light on the fourth floor. She paused and took a couple of deep breaths, her eyes searching for the next stairway. But at the place where it was supposed to be, there was nothing but a balustrade and a blank wall. The stairs didn't go any higher. She took a cautious look down over the edge. The stairs beneath her dissolved into the darkness. Was she already at the top? She listened with great concentration. It still seemed as if the music was coming from higher up.

She turned around and peered down the hallway. It looked just like the hall on the second floor, with a door exactly in the same position as her bedroom door. The only turned-on light was right next to it. Perhaps she could listen for a minute at the window in this room. From up here, it should be easier to hear the direction the music was coming from. She pulled down the door handle and waited. Nothing happened. Cautiously, she stuck her head inside.

The room was dark. It smelled musty. She pushed the door open a little further and walked in. The light of the neon letters enabled her to find a little lamp next to the bed, and she turned it on.

The room wasn't much different from hers, except everything here was covered in yellow flowers instead of pink. The bed had not been slept in. Wherever she looked, there was a layer of dust.

The window was so dirty that she couldn't see through it. She cautiously pulled on the handle. It wouldn't budge. She tugged once more, this time with both hands. Suddenly, the window shot up just a little, rattling loudly. Startled, she took a step backward. The piano stopped in the middle of a passage.

Not daring to breathe, she waited.

In the silence, she heard another sound from outside. Bending down, she tried to look out the window. The opening was just big enough for her head and shoulders.

Something was moving near the bus down below. With relief, she recognized Dantzig scurrying back and forth. His white fur kept flashing pink. She opened her mouth to call to him but changed her mind. If she wanted the piano to start up again, it was probably better to keep quiet. With her chin in her hands, she leaned on the windowsill and stared at the hill in the distance.

Behind her came a loud crash.

She jerked her head up, bumping it against the window. With the crash still ringing in her ears, she turned around.

The draft coming in the open window had caused the door to slam shut. She heaved a sigh of relief while rubbing the sore spot on her head, and then hurried over to the door. All of a sudden, she didn't feel like waiting for the piano anymore.

She wanted to get back to her own room right away. *Tomorrow I'll pick up where I've left off,* she thought, and pushed the handle down.

The door didn't open.

She grabbed the handle with both hands, jerking and pulling with all her might. It wouldn't budge. The door remained closed.

Maybe something jammed when the door slammed shut, she thought. Nervously, she jiggled the handle, up and down, left and right. Did she hear something? Out in the hall?

She stopped and listened. Then she bent down and tried to look through the keyhole. It was too dark in the hall to see anything. Or was the keyhole being blocked?

"Hello?" She said it softly at first. And then, right away, she said it again, louder. "Hello! Is anybody there? I'm locked in!"

There was no answer. She held her breath and pressed her ear against the door. Now she heard a low buzzing noise, like a machine slowly gaining speed. The sound continued for ten, fifteen, twenty seconds. Then it stopped.

She jerked and pulled on the handle again and pounded on the door with both fists. Then she hurried back to the window and stuck out her head.

"Dantzig!" she called down. "Are you there?"

No answer. She called again. Maybe he had just gone inside for a minute.

"Keep calm," she whispered. "I have to keep calm." She pulled a chair right up next to the window and sat on the edge. Every now and then, she leaned forward to see if Dantzig had come outside yet. She closed her eyes and rocked back and forth. *There's absolutely nothing to worry about,* she thought. *Any minute now, Dantzig will come out.*

But she was too restless to sit still. She walked past the bed and back again, stood in front of the mirror, and tried to smile at herself. It was a tearful smile. She had to try to think of something else.

"I've got my name back," she said out loud to the mirror. "Mouse." The second smile was more successful. Her reflection smiled back. You see? Nothing to worry about.

"And I think best with my elbows on my knees ..." She nodded. Things were already looking up. "I have a red raincoat ..." What else? "I can play the piano ..."

I'm in here and I can't get out, came flashing through her mind. Don't think about it!

"I have a bag full of music books." And a key on a chain, she suddenly remembered. She felt around in her pants pocket and pulled it out. Then she held it under the light so she could examine the pendant. It looked like ... a house? But a house with a roof that was much too big.

She didn't have enough patience to look at it very long. Her gaze strayed off toward the door. Why wouldn't it open?

"Stop thinking about it this instant!" she said severely to her reflection in the mirror. But her thoughts wouldn't listen anymore and went their own way, tumbling around through her head.

Why hadn't her reflection laughed back? Why didn't the animals answer her questions? And what was she looking for here anyway?

She tried the door once again. It still wouldn't budge. Feeling restless, she walked to the window and leaned out. Where was Dantzig? What if he had gone to sleep?

The lights on the roof just kept on flashing. Suddenly, she couldn't understand how they could have made her laugh earlier tonight. She lay down in bed, her back to the window so she wouldn't have to look at them anymore. Shivering, she pulled the blankets up around her. She was so tired. ...

She held up the keychain and looked at it, turning it around. Now she saw what it was! It was a little boat. A tiny little boat with a chimney. Or maybe it was a mast.

Grasping the keychain firmly in her hand, and with the blankets wrapped tightly around her, she began to calm down. She closed her eyes for a moment. Slowly, her breathing became even.

Dear, incredibly big daughter of mine,

Have you ever had the feeling that time wasn't sticking to the rules? That the minutes just weren't following each other in a nice, neat, orderly way? How else can you explain the fact that another whole year has gone by? A year of seeing way too little of you ...

I'm starting to sound loony. That's because for almost two days we've been stuck in a place where time doesn't seem to exist.

When you read this letter, your birthday will probably be over. But as I write, it's still not here. So you may already know what I'm going to tell you when you open the letter. Because it would take a miracle for me to get home in time for your birthday, much as I want to.

I can only tell you how it happened. That's doesn't help, I know. But it's a strange story, and maybe you'll enjoy reading it in spite of everything.

It all started with the boat breaking down. Fortunately, we could still reach the harbor in Trieste. That's where we are now. It's so depressing: the condition of the boat, the condition of my heart. We have to wait here for parts. And even then, there's a chance they won't be able to get it back in working order. That's why I have to stay here. After all, it is my boat.

We managed to lay our hands on an old bus in exchange

for a couple of performances on the harbor square. The bus was standing here on the wharf, rusting away. An antique Paris city bus. While waiting for the parts, we decided to drive around the neighborhood, to make a little money by playing. But late one night, in the pitch-dark, the old thing just up and died. We were far away from the civilized world, so we all slept in the bus. In the morning, when it started to get light (that was yesterday), we discovered we were right next to an abandoned hotel! It's so abandoned that there's no public transportation for miles around and not even a mailbox!

Fortunately, there is a handyman here who says he can get the bus going again. We've promised him that if he's able to get us back to the harbor in the bus, he can keep it. If his stick-to-itiveness is anything to go by, we should be back soon. He's already taken apart the whole engine twice.

Today I started on your story. If I ever get back to civilization again (and I just heard the engine roar, so there's still hope), I'll send it along with this letter. Then at least I will have kept a little bit of my promise: that you would receive the beginning of the story on your birthday.

I'm curious to hear what you think of it. I hope you'll want to take it further in the meantime.

Last night, my trumpet and I climbed the only hill in the area. And from there, we tooted all the birthday songs I could think of in your direction. If we're still here tonight, I'll do it again. And if you don't hear it—and that's not likely, because I have strong lungs and you have excellent ears—please know that I'm thinking of you and I'm doing my very best to get back to you as soon as I can. Make sure you have a terrific birthday so you can tell me all about it later on.

I'm sending you twenty-two kisses, eleven for each cheek.

Your father

P.S.: If you want to write back, send your letter general delivery to Trieste. I'll check in at the post office every day until we leave.

A dry click. And another. Was she dreaming? Mouse did her best to regain consciousness.

I've got to get up, she thought sleepily, but she was too groggy to move.

She yawned. With her free hand, she pulled the blankets up higher. There was that piano music again. And what was all that thumping? It seemed to be coming from right over her head. *That can't be,* she thought drowsily. There *is* nothing overhead. There aren't even any stairs... .

So I am dreaming, she thought. And even before she could yawn again, she had sunk back into a deep sleep.

You see—there are more stairs! She just hadn't looked carefully enough. Where do all those stairs go anyway? They go higher and higher, with no end in sight... . And what's all that rustling in the distance—or is it giggling? She can't hear very well because the piano music keeps on playing... . Pipe down, she wants to shout, then at least I'll be able to hear what that rustling is. But she needs all her breath for climbing. In the distance, two restless balcony doors keep flapping open and shut. The closer she gets, the smaller the opening becomes. She can just barely fit through, and that's only because she's holding her breath. The doors close right behind her with a sigh. There's the piano. Of course! Why hadn't she looked there before?

Its high back is facing her. She can't see if anyone is sitting on the bench. Now that the music has stopped, the rustling is more distinct: It's coming from the other side of the piano, except now it sounds more like sniffing. She wants to tiptoe around the piano, but it's a long way, much farther than it looks. Stop dawdling, Sleepyhead, two voices call out, one high and one low. Or can't you find it? Sitting on the piano keys are two white mice with their backs to each other. Or are they rats? You really have to learn how to look at things, they shout out in chorus, their little red eyes gleaming angrily. Never seen a mouse and a rat before? Now she can tell the difference: One is much bigger, with longer whiskers sticking out every which way.

Well. Was that so difficult? shouts the rat. As soon as they start running over the keys, the music starts up again. The mouse runs forward, and the rat lurches backward behind her. The keys of the music climb higher and higher. The rat starts pulling in the opposite direction; the keys go lower. Now the mouse has to run backward to keep up. I didn't realize piano keys were so big, pants the mouse. She has to lift her feet up high to get from one key to the next. Don't pull so, she shouts with a strange, high voice. How did she get that high voice, anyway? Because I myself am that mouse, she discovers with a shock.

So what? Nothing odd about that, says the rat behind her. I myself am a rat, right? Should I tell you a secret? Actually, I'm not an ordinary rat anymore. That's because now I've got a name, except I've forgotten what it is.

Pulling with all her might, she tries to go forward. But the harder she pulls, the further back she gets dragged over the keys. She twists around until she can see behind her. Then she understands why she can't make any headway: The rat's fleshy pink tail is tied to hers with a graceful bow in the middle and a double knot on top. She tries to scream, but no sound comes from her throat.

Stop! I've had just about enough of that, the rat shouts sternly. Stop! he shouts again.

What do you mean? What am I doing? she wants to ask, but the rat drowns her out: You're ruining everything! I've had just about enough of you!

Mouse sat up with her head in a fog. Pale morning light was filling the room. The bedside lamp was still on. In her sleep, she had kicked the blanket to the foot of the bed; now it was knotted around her legs. Outside she heard a dull thud.

"If this doesn't stop RIGHT NOW, I'll, I'll ..."

Finally, she managed to free her feet. She rolled out of bed and hurried to the window.

Down below, Dantzig was climbing onto the hood of the bus. From there, he jumped onto the roof, where he picked something up and threw it with a wave of his arm. A spot remained on the roof of the bus that looked as if something had spattered there. She couldn't see what it was from that height, only that there were several spots.

"WAIT a minute!" Dantzig jabbed the air with his fist in fury. He bent over and carefully rubbed away the spots. Only when the roof began to gleam again, did he slide back down.

"What is it?" Fermer's head popped out from a window right below Mouse.

Mouse couldn't understand Dantzig's answer, but she could tell how angry he was because he was tripping over his tongue. He picked up a cloth that was lying in the sand next to the bus. She recognized the yellow-flowered fabric from the sheet on her bed. Fermer's low voice responded quietly.

"What do you mean, ignore it?" Dantzig screamed, interrupting him. He shook the cloth out with a snap and laid it on the ground near the bus next to a blue cloth that was already there, carefully pulling the corners straight.

"You know very well what I mean." Fermer began speaking louder, too.

Curious, Mouse leaned out further. Wasn't that her room, where Fermer was hanging out of the window? She stood up with a shock. Only now did she remember the door. How could she have forgotten!

She quickly slid the window shut, ran through the room, and grabbed the handle. The door opened easily. Much relieved, she looked out into the hall. Go! Go! Go! She ran down the two flights of stairs to the second floor. The door to her room was slightly ajar.

She entered as Fermer was closing the balcony doors.

"Mouse! Where were you?" He looked at her reproachfully. "I was so hoping that today I'd be on time to serve you breakfast in bed." Disappointed, he gestured from the tray at the foot of her bed to the place where she should have been lying.

"I was upstairs," said Mouse. She picked up her bag, which had slid from the bedside table to the floor. One of the books had fallen halfway out. She pushed it back into the bag and placed the bag on the bed.

"Upstairs?" Fermer asked with surprise. "What were you doing up there?" He picked up the tray and walked to the door.

"I wanted to find out where the music was coming from." Mouse followed right behind him. "I was just looking around, and suddenly I got locked in."

"Locked in?" He turned, deeply alarmed, and studied her carefully.

"The door of one of the rooms slammed shut, and I couldn't get it open."

She pointed upward. "It was right overhead. But it worked fine just now, all of a sudden."

"Dear girl!" Fermer said in a worried voice. Holding the tray in front of him, he walked down the hall. Then he peered up the stairs and shook his head.

"The door must have slammed shut in the wind, and that's what made it stick. I'll tell Dantzig to have a look at the lock," he said, and started walking down the stairs.

"What about that music?" asked Mouse. She was walking right behind him. "Where's that coming from?"

Fermer only shrugged his shoulders.

"I'm glad you didn't hurt yourself." He waited in the lobby below until Mouse got to the door of the waiting room and held it open for him. "Everything upstairs has been neglected for such a long time ... maybe it's better not to go up there." He walked around the bar and looked at her.

"Too bad about that breakfast in bed, though. Maybe tomorrow!" He put the tray down on the bar with a regretful sigh. On the tray was a plate with a stack of crepes. Mouse looked for the least burned one, rolled it up, and gobbled it down in a couple of bites. When she looked up, Fermer had already disappeared through the swinging doors.

She rolled up a second crepe and went outside with it, searching for Dantzig. She didn't see him near the bus, so she walked around the corner. Maybe he was in his workshop? The door was open a crack.

"Dantzig?" She stuck her head in the door. There was no answer.

She shoved the rest of the crepe into her mouth and slipped

through the crack into the gloom. Her eyes had to adjust to the darkness before she could see the lightbulb dangling above her with its little cord. She pulled on the cord. And at that very moment, someone behind her gave her a shove. Losing her balance, she fell forward into the armchair. Then she felt herself being grabbed by the shoulders.

"How dare you!" screamed a voice, distorted with rage. "How dare you come in here!"

Mouse wanted to look behind her, but she couldn't move because her face was pushed against the chair. She could hardly breathe. And with her mouth so full of crepe, she wasn't able to scream. She swallowed the wrong way and started coughing violently.

Someone pulled her up. Finally, she was able to turn her head.

Behind her stood Dantzig. His eyes were dark with anger.

"Snooping around, huh? As if nothing—"

He stopped in mid-sentence.

"Mouse!?" He stared at her in confusion. From one minute to the next, his anger evaporated. "Is that you?"

Deeply embarrassed, he let her go and looked her over from head to foot. "What are you doing here?"

"I wasn't snooping around at all!" Mouse swallowed the last bit of crepe and took a step backward, seething with indignation. "I was just looking for you." It was as if Dantzig's anger was contagious.

"But if that's the way you're going to act, then FORGET IT!" She stared at him, fuming. She opened her mouth to say something else. But she was so angry, she couldn't get the words out. So she turned and left, bounding past him and through the door.

THIS IS A LETTER BOMB! If you don't show up for my birthday, you're the ROTTENEST father I know, and I don't ever want to see you again. Of course I SHOULDN'T have believed you when you solemnly PROMISED to come home THIS TIME ESPECIALLY for my birthday. And why did it take you so long to write? If you had written earlier, at least I wouldn't have stood there at the bus station waiting for you LIKE AN IDIOT. The fact that they don't have a mailbox out there in that drippy jungle is just a LOUSY EXCUSE. And one more thing: I'm sending back that stupid story of yours. If that's the kind of story it's going to be, then FORGET IT. I lost interest in the whole idea a long time ago. It's CHILDISH anyway. Talking animals. Don't you even know how old I'm going to be? I'm going to be ELEVEN, not FOUR! But how would you know that, if you're NEVER HERE. What good are you as a father? If that STUPID BOAT of yours is so much more important, JUST STAY THERE AND GOOD RIDDANCE!

"Mouse! Wait! I'm sorry!" Dantzig ran after her. "I didn't mean it like that!" Just before the corner, he caught up with her and blocked her way.

"I was mistaken! I just thought—" He caught himself and fell silent. Then he brushed some imaginary dust from her clothes and straightened her sweater. "I didn't hurt you, did I?"

"*What* did you just think?" Mouse put her hands on her hips impatiently.

"I was wrong. I'm sorry." He blinked. "It's the tension. It makes me do strange things. It's because ..." He began to giggle nervously, grabbing her arm and gesturing toward the bus. Reluctanctly, Mouse let him pull her along.

"Today I'm going to try to put the engine back together!" He didn't let go of her until they got to the bus, where he made a strange, little jump. Spread out on the cloths next to the bus was the entire engine, broken down into separate parts. Mouse looked at it grudgingly. *Why on earth had he taken apart the engine? So many little bits,* she thought with irritation. *How could anyone ever make any sense out of it?*

"I'm sorry I scared you like that." Dantzig tore his gaze away from the cloths. "It really won't happen again. My solemn promise." He laid one paw on her arm and grinned sheepishly.

"Promise?" The word caused her anger to flare up once

more. She stamped her foot in the sand. Dantzig let go of her arm and took a step backward.

"You already promised you'd get that bus fixed. Or have you forgotten?" In her rage, she stumbled over her words. "And bragging that you'd get it started … just look at it now." She nodded indignantly at the cloths.

"You'll never get anywhere with that." She hardly heard what she was saying herself. Dantzig tried to get a word in edgewise, but the last thing she wanted to do was listen to him.

"And even if you did make it work, do you really think anyone would be crazy enough to go for a ride in that rattletrap?" She folded her arms, curious to hear what he had to say to that.

Dantzig didn't say a word. He just gazed at her with a strange look in his eye. Then he turned around, walked to the front of the bus, stepped onto the box, and disappeared with his head under the hood.

I stamp up the four flights of stairs as loud as I can. The apartment door is still ajar. In my rush to go out, I had left it open.

"Back again?"

It's Robin's voice calling from the kitchen. I follow it unwillingly.

"Where did you go all of a sudden?"

"Mail a letter." I lean against the doorpost and watch her pour the batter for my birthday cake from a bowl into a cake tin.

"To Sky?" Robin puts the tin in the oven and picks up the timer. "That was fast." She gives me a searching glance. I avoid her eyes. The timer starts ticking impatiently.

"Want to lick the bowl?" She holds it up.

I shake my head and turn away. In the living room, I pick up my book from the blue chair. Before Robin can say another word, I hurry across the hall to the mini-room and shut the door behind me.

As hard as I can, I kick away the wad of paper lying on the floor. It bounces off the wall and shoots back, landing at the foot of my bed. Rotten letter! I drop onto my bed, not even opening the book. I'm much too angry to read.

They're all rotten letters! All of them! It's not the first time he hasn't done what he promised. Furious, I pull the stack of letters out from under my bed. How many times did he write to say he was coming home later, or that he had to leave earlier? I pull out one letter after another, so roughly that one of them rips in half. It's a nice sound; it makes me even angrier. I grab another and rip it down the middle, and then another. I grab a couple of them together and pull until they rip, too, again and again. The harder it is to get them to rip, the better. I can't stop myself. And they're all covered with spots from these rotten tears. I keep on going till there's nothing left but shreds. My bed is snowed under.

I brush away my tears and stare stupidly at the white flakes all around me. It's as if I had suddenly woken up. What have I done?

I drop onto my back so I don't have to look at the mess. A seagull flies past over the skylight. I can hear it screaming.

"Honey?" Robin calls from the kitchen.

Startled, I scramble up, grope for the scraps of paper, and jam them by the handful into the white bag lying at the foot of my bed. There's a moving box on the floor of the closet. I bury the bag at the very bottom, under the old stuffed animals that are already lying there because I don't need them anymore anyway.

Then I grab my book, drop onto the bed, and pretend to be reading.

Mouse gazed uneasily at Dantzig's back. His tail hung down heavily over the box. The way he had looked at her just now dissolved her anger in a stroke. Suddenly, she couldn't remember why she had been so furious.

A bit ashamed, she stared at the cloths with the engine parts lying on it. Several metal rings were polished so clean that they glistened in the sun. Two neat rows of gears lay one above the other. The upper row was ordered according to size, from smallest on the left to largest on the right. Beneath it was a similar row, but these gears went from large to small, so the two rows together formed a big rectangle. Everything was carefully arranged. Each part was exactly where it had to be. The longer she looked, the more ashamed she felt about the things she'd said.

She bent over and picked up the smallest gear. Her pinky fit right into the hole in the middle.

"Dantzig?"

There was no answer. She turned the gear around and around.

"I didn't mean what I said."

No answer. A ring of black grease formed around her pinky. She put back the gear and walked to the hood of the bus.

"I really do believe you're going to do it."

Did she hear grumbling?

"And I don't think your bus is stupid at all. In fact, it's beautiful." The grumbling stopped. Filled with hope, she moved one step closer. "I'm sorry. I was just so scared."

A bang came from under the hood. Dantzig cursed loudly. She froze in her tracks.

"Everything okay?" she asked anxiously.

Dantzig straightened himself up with a jerk. "Miserable screw! What's the matter with it?" He gave her a haggard look. His head was streaked with black. "Every time I try to turn it, that thing falls out!" He waved his screwdriver around helplessly, like a conductor who had lost his orchestra.

Mouse climbed up on the box beside him and looked curiously over the edge. She sniffed the odor of oil and gasoline. There was an enormous hole where the engine was supposed to be. With the point of his screwdriver, Dantzig poked at a metal plate that was dangling from a single little screw.

"Should I give it a try?" Mouse stuck out her hand.

"Do you know anything about engines?" Dantzig looked at her suspiciously, but he put the screw in her hand.

Mouse pretended to turn the question over in her mind, and then shrugged her shoulders. "I don't know."

She stuck out her other hand. Dantzig sighed. Reluctantly, he released the screwdriver.

Mouse bent forward. Dantzig leaned over so far that his whiskers tickled her cheek and she could hardly see the hole for that particular screw. With the tip of her tongue almost touching her nose, she pushed the screw carefully into place. Just before it fell out again, she caught it with the screwdriver, turning it slowly until it was tightened.

"Will you look at that!" Dantzig started giggling with astonishment. "Nothing to it for those skinny, little fingers!"

Mouse stood up and stared at her dirty hands with satisfaction. The last bit of orange on her fingers had disappeared under the black grease.

"You got any more of those screws?" she asked.

Dantzig scratched behind his ear. "Now that you mention it ... I could use an extra pair of paws today. Especially, if they're clever ones like yours."

His eyes were gleaming again. He jumped off the box and ran over to the engine parts. Mouse followed him with relief, happy she could do something for him. And especially happy that he wasn't angry with her anymore.

There's a faint knock on the door.

"Honey?" Robin looks in through a crack in the door. I hide my head behind my book. She comes in and sits down on the edge of the bed. It takes a while before she says anything.

"There's nothing Sky would rather do than be with his daughter on her eleventh birthday. You know that, don't you?"

"Oh, yeah?" I turn toward her, seething with rage. "Then why isn't he here?"

"The boat broke down. It's just bad luck. He's got to stay there. As soon as there's any way to leave, he'll come back." She puts a hand on my shoulder. I shake it off angrily. I don't understand why she always has to stand up for him.

"You know how important the orchestra is, and the boat? Not only for your father, but for us, too. And for the other musicians. A whole lot of people depend on it." She pauses. I don't answer. I've heard this all so many times before.

"Is that his letter?" She points to the wad of paper at the foot of my bed. "May I read it?"

I shrug my shoulders. She goes ahead.

She unfolds the paper and flattens it out as smooth as she can. For a moment, there's silence. I can hear the kitchen timer along with the ticking of the oven as it heats up.

"Is it nice?" Robin asks when she's done. "The story?"

I shrug my shoulders again. This time because I don't know what to say.

"May I see that, too?"

"No. It's stupid. And childish." She doesn't have to know that I sent it back with my angry letter.

For a while, Robin just sits there looking at me and doesn't say a word. I stare sullenly at the clouds through the skylight. The smell of the freshly baked cake slowly begins to drift through the room.

"We're going to have a fantastic birthday tomorrow." She smiles; I can just see it from the corner of my eye. "And when Sky comes home, we'll just celebrate it all over again."

She folds up the wrinkled paper carefully.

"Save this with the others, why don't you." She holds the letter in the air above my bellybutton. "Before it catches fire from those red-hot eyes of yours." She smiles again and lets it go. I can feel it land through my T-shirt, so gently it almost tickles. But after a while, it feels like a stone lying on my stomach.

"What's that smell?" Dantzig stuck his nose in the air and gave an attentive sniff.

Now Mouse could smell it, too. The sweet smell of freshly baked pastry. She straightened up and looked around. The sun had crossed the sky and was now hovering just over the roof of the hotel. How long had she been working?

"We can still set the points before it gets too dark." Dantzig held up a couple of scraps of paper. "The distance between these things has to be very precise. Two pieces of paper is exactly the right thickness. I figured it out once." He pushed the scraps into Mouse's hand and showed her just where to hold them.

"Don't move …" He groaned from the effort. "That ought to do it." He let out his breath with a whistling sound. "Pretty handy, huh? Okay, take them out! Great stuff, that paper." He briskly straightened himself up.

Mouse pulled her arms out of the engine. They were covered with black grease way past the elbows. She jumped from the box onto the sand and looked at the cloths with satisfaction. Almost all the parts were gone.

Out of the waiting room came Fermer, carrying a full tray. He walked with quick, mincing steps as if he could barely lift it, and approached the bus with a gentle, tinkling sound.

"That's enough for today." Dantzig stood next to her and

wiped off his paws on a dingy rag. "You were a tremendous help." He looked at her happily. Suddenly, he bent over and gave her a kiss on the cheek. His whiskers scratched. Mouse shyly looked at her hands, trying to fold the pieces of paper smaller and smaller.

Dantzig chuckled. He handed her the rag and started putting away his tools. She did her best to rub the oil from her fingers, but she only smeared the black spots and made them bigger.

Fermer kicked a few screws aside with his hind foot and put the tray on the yellow-flowered cloth. He got to work setting out the plates and glasses, so the cloth suddenly turned into a picnic blanket. In the middle, he put a big pitcher of lemonade, a plate of flat, round cookies, and a platter of sandwiches.

Mouse sat leaning against the bus. She picked up a sandwich and took a cautious nibble. It was so hard she could scarcely bite into it. Dantzig sat down beside her, holding sandwiches in each paw, nibbling one first and then the other. It was easy with his sharp teeth. After each bite, he nodded his head. Mouse pushed her sandwich toward him as inconspicuously as she could and tried a cookie. There were nuts in it.

"Delicious!" She looked at the fox with surprise. "Your cooking is much better today than it was yesterday."

Dantzig finished his sandwiches and crammed a nut cookie into his mouth, grumbling in agreement.

"I had completely forgotten how nice it is to cook for guests." Somewhat bashfully, Fermer filled the glasses to the brim and sat down on the other side of Mouse.

"I'm thinking," he said hesitantly, "about giving a dinner tomorrow." He stared attentively at his glass, put it down, and leaned back. "And I think I'll make something with chanterelles." It took a minute before he could continue because he had to yawn.

"We got a lot more done today than I thought we would." Dantzig loudly slurped the rest of his lemonade. "From now on, things are really going to pick up around here." He licked the inside of his glass clean.

"I've also found a couple of jars of chick peas. Perhaps I can do something with them. Or maybe lentils? But how long do they have to soak?" Fermer yawned again.

"Fortunately, the piston rings are still in good shape, because I sure don't know how I'd get hold of new ones." Dantzig leaned back like Fermer and started snoring immediately.

Mouse ate her third nut cookie with pitch-black hands. It was fun helping Dantzig. She glanced over at him. He seemed so sloppy. But when it came to engines, he knew exactly where everything was supposed to go. She hadn't thought about anything else all afternoon. She leaned back between the two animals, deeply satisfied, and shut her eyes. For a while, no one said a word.

Fermer was the first to move. Groaning quietly, he straightened himself up. "Either today or tomorrow, something really has to be done about the waiting room door," he muttered in mid-stretch. "It almost fell off its hinges this afternoon."

That made Mouse think about the neon lights. "Have you two noticed that not all the letters are working?" She pointed up to the roof.

"That's something for Dantzig." Fermer started stacking the plates.

"Two of them are out." Mouse turned to Dantzig.

"Hmm ..." He brushed aside her words without opening his eyes.

"Maybe that's why there are no other guests," said Mouse. Suddenly, she remembered that Dantzig couldn't read. "You know what the sign says now, when it's on? It says—"

"If two lights are out," Dantzig said abruptly, "then three are still working. So most of them are all right." He jumped up, rummaged noisily through the tool chest, and started walking toward his workshop.

Mouse watched him uncertainly. Had she said something wrong? She looked beseechingly at Fermer.

"The lighting is a rather sensitive issue." Fermer winked at her. "Doesn't matter. He'll forget it in no time." He put the glasses on top of everything else and walked back to the waiting room, with the tray tinkling gently.

The sun had sunk behind the hotel. Giant shadow letters appeared at her feet. She stood there, not knowing what to do. Would Dantzig come outside again? Each time it surprised her how quickly his mood could change. She didn't understand what she had said about the letters that upset him. Her eyes moved up along the front of the building. At that very moment, the three letters went on. They stood out bright pink against the evening sky.

Just below the T, a piece of curtain fluttered outside. She narrowed her eyes. It was the room in the middle, above hers.... That must be the room where she had been locked in the night before. She watched with curiosity as the flowered fabric waved out through the balcony doors and back in again. Who had opened them?

She took another hesitant look toward the workshop. Then she shrugged, turned around, and hurried inside.

The hum of the sewing machine is coming from the living room.

"What you making?" I peer around the corner of the door, wondering what she's up to.

"A late birthday present." Robin holds up something white. "Almost done."

It's a new bag! Exactly the same as my old one.

"I actually thought you were right yesterday."

I look at her, not really knowing what she means.

"When I asked about your bag." She raises her eyebrows. "You said you weren't using it anymore because it was worn out."

I nod, a bit hesitantly. What I had told her wasn't the whole truth.

"It really has seen better days. You've had it so long." She smiles. "And you without your bag, it's just ... odd." She clips a couple of loose threads and turns the bag inside out. I stand there uneasily and watch her. At the same time, it makes me happy. I throw my arms around her neck and give her a kiss. She gives me a sideways glance.

"My big girl ... I can hardly believe it's eleven years already since we had you."

"Eleven years and four days." I sit down in the blue chair, happy that she's changed the subject. "Tell me again how I came to be." I pull up my knees.

Robin looks at the ceiling and sighs deeply, but she smiles at the same time. She's told this story a hundred times before.

"I had a chance to fill in with a choir that had just started touring with the orchestra your father was playing in. But I didn't know him then." She starts pinning down the strap. I like to look at her fingers. They're so fast and graceful.

"The only one I knew a little was Malakoff. He came to pick me up at the station in Paris. He had brought a fellow musician with him." She feeds the fabric into the machine and bends forward. "That was Sky." The machine hums.

"When the choir went home, his orchestra kept on touring. But a few weeks later—"

"You're making it much too short," I shout indignantly. "That's no way to tell it!"

"I don't have time for the unabridged version right now! I want to go over to the new house to measure the window frames." She pulls the bag out from under the needle, turns it over, and feeds it back in.

"But you're skipping all the nice parts!" I protest.

I mean the romantic parts. About love at first sight, and that they wandered together through the streets of all the cities they went to. That they took endless walks, and that Sky talked about his plan to start his own orchestra.

But Robin is unrelenting.

"When he showed up at my door a couple of weeks later, we both had news. He said he'd given up his job with the orchestra and had bought an old boat that he was going to fix up."

She steps on the pedal and the machine hums.

"And I told him that you were on the way." The machine starts humming again.

"Malakoff was one of the musicians who was brave enough

to switch to the new orchestra. Because we had so little money, he offered to let us live here in the attic of his house. In exchange, I would take care of the house and the other tenants when he was traveling. We could just about manage that way." She clips the last thread and holds up the bag.

"Done!" She tosses it over to me. It makes an arc and lands right on my lap. She looks at me, suddenly serious, as she holds the cord of the machine in her hand.

"Do you see why he can't just abandon that boat? And how it doesn't mean that the boat is more important than you are?"

This makes me think about my angry letter. Would Sky have gotten it by now? Something else I haven't told Robin. First there was my birthday, and then the party, and then ... I was ashamed to think about it. Actually, I regret it already. And why did I send back the story? I was so angry, I hadn't even read it very carefully. I just hope he saves it. Or sends it back. If he ever writes back, that is.

Robin is standing in the hall. She sticks her head around the door. Should I tell her? Hesitantly, I open my mouth.

"I'm leaving soon." She already has her coat on. "They're bringing over the rest of the moving boxes this afternoon. Stay home till they're here, okay?" She waves hurriedly. Her head disappears without waiting for an answer.

"Mom?" I shout as I hear the front door open.

Her head appears again.

"Thanks for the bag." I've got it hanging in the usual way, the strap diagonally across my chest.

"No problem." She winks cheerfully. "I'm glad you look like you again."

Mouse pushed down the handle and waited. When nothing happened, she opened the door a crack and peered inside. The window was shut. No one was there. Surprised, she opened the door further and stepped inside.

The blanket lay rumpled at the foot of the bed, exactly as she had left it that morning. There was no indication that someone had been here a few minutes before. Or had she been mistaken about the room? She had seen it clearly, though: It was the room in the middle, above her own.

She walked into the hall and opened the next door. There was an identical room behind it with the same dusty furniture. Everything looked as if no one had been there for ages. She shrugged her shoulders, closed the door, and walked on to the next. At least now she could try to find out where that piano was.

Behind every door was a room with the same yellow flowery furniture. All the beds were smoothly made up and undisturbed. Everything was covered with a thick layer of dust, and nowhere did she find a piano. Was it one floor lower after all?

She crept quietly down the stairs. On the third floor, the furniture in every room was green instead of yellow, but it was just as dusty. And there was no piano here, either. Deeply puzzled, she went down to the second floor and checked out all the rooms there just to be sure. They were all as pink as hers. It didn't surprise her not to find a piano on that floor. The sound was clearly coming from somewhere up above.

If there is someone here who plays the piano, then he's doing his very best to keep from being found, she said to herself with disappointment. She shut the last door behind her and went back to her room. Then she turned on the bedside lamp and stared at her greasy hands.

I'm going to take a bath, she decided. *That always makes me happy.* In the bathroom, she turned on the faucets full-blast and threw her clothes over a chair. The key fell out of her pants pocket with a thud—along with something else. She bent over and picked up two tiny bits of paper. Dantzig's little scraps. She had forgotten to give them back.

She sat down on the edge of the tub and unfolded them. They had been written on, one in blue pen and the other in pencil. The wrinkles and grease marks left by her fingers made them difficult to read.

around. I
were, you an
Remember, the
beautifully you play
had climbed very far. As
the tune of the Stair Climber's Song.
dancer? (And that dancing is a great

understand. So wha
ree or four times befo
me instead! After all, I'm
wo hotheads who would be bet

The handwriting looked the same on both the scraps. What a strange g ... it looked like a pair of eyeglasses standing on their side with a twisted cord hanging down. It was a letter that you only saw in books. Who in the world would write a g like that?

The tub began to fill up. She returned the bits of paper to her pants pocket and put the pants back on the chair. *It's all very strange,* Mouse thought as she settled into the warm water. Dantzig couldn't read or write... . She picked up a bar of soap and tried to scrub the black grease from her arms. So how did he get that paper? She put down the soap and turned off the faucets. When the splashing stopped, she could hear the piano in the distance.

This time, it wasn't the song that went up and down. This time, it sounded different. As if someone were working on a new piece: each time a few measures, first one hand and then the other, then both hands together. Just long enough until it sounded good, and then on to the next part. *That's the way I always did it,* Mouse said to herself. The more the separate parts grew together, the more it began sounding like a real melody. The music gave her a good feeling. Without thinking about it, she sang along for a while.

How did she know the melody went like that? She listened to herself, flabbergasted. Suddenly, she had an idea. She quickly stood up, grabbed a pink towel from the stack, and wrapped it around herself. Then she picked up her bag from the bed, shook out the books, and counted them. She counted them a second time just to make sure. Both times, there were eight. Yesterday morning in the lobby, she had counted nine books. One was missing.

When she came downstairs this morning, her bag had been lying on the floor. Maybe that door up there hadn't slammed shut by accident after all last night. Maybe someone had shut it on purpose so they could look around her room without being disturbed. Maybe that someone had taken a piece of music from her bag.

Maybe, she thought hopefully as she picked up the pink pajamas from the bed, *that person wasn't trying very hard not to be found.* She jumped into the pajamas and opened the door. Only then, did she notice that the music had stopped. Leaning against the doorpost, she waited to see if it would start up again.

In the silence, she heard the same buzzing sound that she had heard last night, as if a machine had started running in the distance. It droned through the hall. Ten seconds, fifteen ... Just like the last time. Right before it stopped, she heard a muffled thud, as if a door—or a hatch—was being slammed somewhere far away. Then it was silent again.

Last night, she had heard it upstairs, on the fourth floor. How could she hear the same sound down here? Suddenly, with irritation, she banged the door shut behind her and fell into bed. She was starting to get fed up with all this searching for things that never got found and questions that never got answered. *If I can't even find a piano in an empty hotel,* she thought despairingly, *how am I going to be able to deal with important things? How will I ever get my memory back?*

She stared at the bag on the pillow next to her and thought about her name. It had come back to her just like that, and she hadn't even worked hard to recall it. What had Dantzig said? Something about not looking for what you're looking for, or was it the other way around?

Maybe, thought Mouse, *it's the same with other things, just like it was with my name.* She wrapped a blanket around her shoulders and rolled herself up in it. Maybe finding things would be easier if I stopped looking for them.

The more purple we put on the wall, the darker it gets. Purple seemed like such a warm color in the paint store. But here, in the basement, it only makes my room look depressing. Especially now that summer is over. Or do I only think that because everything is depressing?

Birdie does the big parts with a roller. I follow her with a brush and do the edges where the roller won't reach. We're just halfway done. Birdie notices how doubtful I look. She takes a step back. "It has to dry first," she says. "Then it may get a little lighter." She hangs the roller in the paint can.

"I'm going to take a look upstairs," she says. I nod and walk silently behind her. Robin is in living room, sitting amid all the moving boxes. She unpacks something, holds it in her hand, and keeps staring at it. This has been going on for quite some time. Sometimes she just puts it back.

"We shouldn't have moved," she says as Birdie sits down beside her. "We should have stayed there."

She says that all the time, too.

"You had no choice. The arrangements were already made." Birdie takes the vase from her hand and puts it on a table. "It's better here. You were bursting at the seams in that attic."

"In the attic, it seemed as if Sky might still come home. But here ..." She takes something else out of the box. She puts it on the table, next to the vase without unwrapping it.

"I keep thinking: He was always going swimming. Nothing ever happened. Why this time?"

"Why do accidents happen?" Birdie sits down next to her and starts unwinding the newspaper. "The weather suddenly changed. Maybe he didn't see it coming. And no one knew he had gone swimming." She puts a second vase next to the first one.

"Constantly asking yourself questions like that" —Birdie balls up the newspaper and throws it in the box— "it doesn't do anybody any good. Least of all you two."

I walk back downstairs as quietly as I can. Robin is right. Sky was always going swimming. He was a good swimmer, wasn't he? What went wrong this time?

I've got an answer all right. I try not to think about it, but my thoughts keep turning in the same direction all by themselves. Something must have happened that kept him from paying attention, from being as careful as he usually was. It couldn't have been a coincidence, could it? That I had just sent him that letter? That he had just ...

I pick up my brush again.

If only I had waited a little longer to write back. Then I wouldn't have been so angry. Or they would already have left the harbor before my letter arrived at the post office. Then it would have just sat there, safe and sound.

That's what I kept on hoping for the first couple of months— that he hadn't received it. If a letter marked "general delivery" isn't picked up within three months, the post office returns it to the sender. I know that for sure. I've had so many letters to Sky returned to me because he hadn't picked them up. But now it's almost four months after the accident, and my letter hasn't come back. I clench my teeth and plunge the brush into the can of paint. A purple blobs splashes over the rim.

The doorbell rings upstairs. I hear Birdie go to open it. A voice murmurs something softly. I can't tell who it is. Someone to see Robin, probably. A little while later, Birdie's footsteps come back down the stairs. When they get to my door, they stop. Why doesn't she come in?

"Nice color," says a hoarse voice. Startled, I let the brush fall from my hands.

"Oh, sweetie! Did I scare you?" Malakoff is standing in the doorway, instead of Birdie. He smiles and cautiously takes a step inside.

"The door was open," said a voice, "or I would have knocked." It was a voice wrapped in a lovely smell. Mouse scrambled up groggily.

"I hope I'm not too early." Fermer stood next to her bed and triumphantly held up a tray. "I just didn't want to be too late again." He looked around for a good place to put it down.

"Was the door open?" Mouse groped for the pillow next to her with one hand. The bag was still there. She rubbed her cheeks and shook her head, trying to get rid of the heaviness.

"Yes. Wide open." Fermer set the tray on top of her legs and poured a cup of tea. Mouse recognized the smell of peppermint. Even that couldn't chase away the nasty feeling. Why did she feel so, so ... sad?

"I didn't know what you would feel like eating." Fermer took a step back and viewed the whole tray critically. "Maybe you don't like scrambled eggs, so I boiled a couple, too. And I made toast, one plain and one with honey."

She nodded and tried to smile. Perhaps she had had a bad dream. But can you get so sad from just one dream?

The bread was too dark on only one side, and the scrambled eggs weren't even too salty. But she just wasn't hungry.

"You're getting better every day," she said, forcing herself to take another bite.

"This is nothing!" Fermer sat down on the edge of the bed. The tea splashed over the side of her cup, but he didn't notice. "I'm really going to get serious when dinner comes." He stared dreamily into space.

Mouse shoved the scrambled eggs back and forth across her plate and pretended to eat.

"I can't make up my mind whether to serve three courses or four. What do you think?" Before she could answer he jumped to his feet. "I say four. Then it really counts." His expression took on a startled look. "I've got to get to work!" On his way to the hall, he did a couple of little dance steps, slamming the door behind him with an elegant sweep.

Relieved, Mouse pushed aside the tray. She grabbed her bag and counted the music books. Seven. If she didn't hide the bag somewhere, they'd all be gone before long. She looked around the room and saw a big closet with a tiny key in the lock. She slipped out of bed and put her bag in the closet. Even the inside of the closet was lined with flowered wallpaper. She turned the key and dropped it in her pants pocket. *Maybe I can go help Dantzig,* she thought as she got dressed. *That's sure to make me feel better.* She picked up the tray and walked carefully downstairs.

The waiting room was empty. Using the tray, she pushed open the swinging doors behind the bar. In the middle of the kitchen was a big table full of dishes and bowls. Above it hung a row of pans, gleaming in the sunlight. Something that smelled vaguely like chocolate was simmering on the stove. Fermer was nowhere to be seen.

Mouse put the tray on the counter and turned around in astonishment. There was the piano again. Here, in the kitchen, it sounded hollow. Listening intently, she circled the room, trying to figure out where the sound was coming from. When she got close to the swinging doors, the sound became louder.

To the left of the doors was a metal hatch built into the wall. 100 LB. MAX. was written on it in black letters. When she pressed her ear to the metal, it felt cold. But right away, she heard the piano much more clearly. She recognized the piece from last night, yet now there were no mistakes. *Yes, that's how it goes,* she said to herself. And before she knew it, she had started to smile. That pianist sure can play... . With her eyes closed, she stood there listening. And for the first time that morning, the heavy feeling began to fade.

There was a big handle at the bottom of the hatch. On the wall next to the hatch was a button with a small red light above it. She pulled on the handle. The hatch didn't move. She pushed the button, but nothing happened. Even the light didn't go on.

"That doesn't do me any good!" Behind the swinging doors, she heard the piercing voice of Dantzig coming closer. "You promised!"

"Unfortunately, I did," Fermer's low voice boomed out. "But sooner or later, it will become obvious." He came through the swinging doors.

"Later is more than soon enough." Dantzig was right behind him. "The later, the better. After all, you don't want—" He stopped in mid-sentence.

"Mouse!" they said in unison, high and low together. They looked at her so sheepishly that she burst out laughing. Fermer hurried to the stove to stir the pan. Dantzig winked at Mouse and dug a handful of nuts from a small bowl. Fermer turned around and threw a towel at him, but Dantzig neatly ducked and slipped out the back door. Fermer watched him, shaking his head.

"Thanks again for breakfast in bed." Mouse pointed to the counter. Suddenly, she realized her appetite had returned. She walked over to the tray and spread a thick layer of cherry jam on the toast with honey. Fermer nodded with satisfaction and started humming a tune. He didn't seem to be able to find the right notes. It sounded more like growling.

"I think I'll do three courses anyway, with some kind of appetizer," he said. He grabbed a cookbook and started thumbing through it. "Four may be too much of a good thing."

The humming started again, even flatter than before. But despite that, she recognized the tune. It was what the piano had played in the beginning. So Fermer heard it, too!

"How about a quiche for starters? It sounds so chic." Fermer took another book from the stack.

"Sounds delicious." Mouse strolled over to the swinging doors. "What kind of a hatch is this, anyway?" she asked.

Fermer looked up from his book with a frown.

"Hatch ... ?" He stared absently to where she was pointing. "Oh—that's an old dumbwaiter—a kind of elevator for transporting food and dishes."

An elevator? Not very big for an elevator. She wondered whether a person could fit inside.

"Will it open?"

Fermer turned a page and shrugged his shoulders.

"Is it broken?" She put the last piece of bread in her mouth.

"No idea. I've never tried it."

"Why not?"

"Don't know. Never needed it." To oblige Mouse, he looked a little longer. "There's a hatch like that on every floor. Maybe it's open somewhere. Only one hatch at a time can be open. I can't decide between yeast dough and puff pastry for the quiche. What do you think?" He opened up a third book and was lost in thought.

On every floor? Mouse remembered her search through the upstairs halls with surprise. Had she overlooked it?

In the silence, she heard the piano start playing again softly. She turned around and pushed open the swinging doors.

"Or is graham cracker crust more to your liking?" Fermer shouted after her.

"Lilac. Nice color." Malakoff picks up the brush and gives it a stroke. It leaves a purple spot on the newspaper.

"You think so?" I take a few steps back. Lilac—it sounds prettier than purple. With this new word in my head, I take another look at the wall. Malakoff comes over and stands beside me. He nods. I'm glad to see him. I haven't been to his house since the funeral and the move right after it.

"I just came from the boat." He rests his hand on my shoulder a minute before sitting down on the edge of my bed. Covered by a plastic sheet to protect it from the paint, it crackles when he moves.

"Your mother had asked me to sort things out there temporarily, as long as her mind is elsewhere. At some point, she'll have to go herself. I also picked up your father's music stuff." He looks at me with his clear gray eyes, which seem to bore right through you. To avoid them, I start painting where I left off, doing my best not to mess up the baseboard.

"I brought something for you." He reaches into his inside pocket. I look up out of curiosity. The plastic on the bed rustles as he pulls out a packet. I recognize it immediately. It's the letters I sent to Sky. In a neat stack, held together with two rubber bands.

"They were in his closet. On the boat." He holds them out

to me. I hesitate. Maybe my angry letter is among them. Instead of taking the stack of letters, I point with my brush to the table next to my bed.

Malakoff looks at me again with that X-ray vision of his and pats the plastic next to him. Reluctantly, I put the brush in the can of paint, come over to him, and sit down.

"I found them like that, with the rubber bands around them. Funny, actually." He turns the package around in his big hands. "Sky was so careless about everything. It drove you nuts." He smiles. "Except with things that were really important to him. His music stuff. Your letters." He puts the stack of letters on the plastic between us.

I nod, but just a little. Malakoff thinks he's helping me, of course, but I'm feeling worse and worse. It makes me think of my old white bag that I haven't yet taken out of the moving box.

"Every time we came into a new port, Sky would go straight to the post office. When he came back, you could tell whether there was a letter from you or not by the way he walked." Malakoff gives me a sideways glance. "Sometimes he'd read parts of them out loud to us, things he thought were funny, or nicely worded. That made him so proud. "

Except for that last letter, I say to myself. Malakoff must have known.

It's quiet for a few minutes.

"You ever play the piano?" he asks suddenly. I shake my head, but I don't say anything because I don't know how to explain it. That I don't feel like playing because Sky can't hear it anymore. He nods thoughtfully, as if I had said it out loud anyway.

"Piano lessons or not, I hope your move doesn't mean you won't come to see me." He stretches out his hand. "After all, it's not *that* far. Even my stiff old legs can walk it in less than fifteen minutes."

I look at his yellow fingers and put my purple hand in his. His hand feels rough and soft at the same time. He puts his other hand on top of mine. It's such a friendly thing to do... . Suddenly, I want to tell him everything. But just when I open my mouth, I hear footsteps coming down the stairs. Birdie looks in and says something about tea being ready, and Robin wanting to discuss a few things with Malakoff.

He gives my hand a quick squeeze before he lets it go. Then he stands up. At the door, he looks around once more.

"If you want to start playing again, come on over! Who else do I have to yell at and come down hard on?" He winks and closes the door behind him.

I keep looking at the packet until Birdie and Malakoff reach the top of the stairs. Then, cautiously, I pick it up. The rubber bands are so tight that they shoot out from under my fingers. I flip through the stack of envelopes.

It's not there.

Just to make sure, I take all the letters out of their envelopes and turn each piece of paper over twice. The letter I wish I hadn't written is not one of them.

I don't know whether to be happy or not.

Is it possible that it just never arrived? That does happen sometimes, right? Filled with hope, I play with that idea for a while. The awful feeling suddenly seems to fade a little. Letters are always getting lost—you hear that all the time!

But maybe not. He threw it away, of course. You don't save a horrible letter like that, do you? The awful feeling settles right back down in place.

I had almost told Malakoff everything! I quickly put the letters back in their envelopes. Before I knew it he would have told Robin ... and she's having such a hard time as it is. I put the first rubber band back on the stack of letters.

With Malakoff around, I'm almost sure I won't be able to keep my secret very long. I listen to the voices talking overhead, feeling very irritated. The second rubber band snaps in the middle and gives my fingers a nasty sting.

I think I'd better stay away from him for the time being.

Now she knew what to look for—and she found it right away. On the second floor, the hatch was just opposite the stairs. The front of the hatch, covered with the same wood as the paneling on the lower half of the wall, was hardly noticeable. It had a small brass handle. She pulled on the handle, but the hatch wouldn't move.

There was an identical hatch in exactly the same place on the third floor. This one wouldn't budge, either, not a single inch. She pressed her ear against it. The pianist had started in on a new piece. It must come from the book that had vanished last night.

When she listened through the hatch on the fourth floor, the sound was even louder. No doubt about it—she was getting closer and closer to the piano. It *had* to be somewhere above her. Leaning back against the hatch, she tried to think. How could the music come out of a dumbwaiter?

She listened to the same passage being played over and over again.

If I could open that hatch, she said to herself, *then I could see where the dumbwaiter goes.*

There was that passage again. The person who was playing kept stumbling over the same few notes. Without giving it a second thought, Mouse whistled a few bars.

The piano stopped abruptly.

Mouse was startled. Had the pianist heard her?

She hesitated, then whistled once more, a little louder this time. Then she waited, her ears straining. The piano slowly repeated her notes, exactly as she had whistled them. Just once. Then silence.

Mouse almost burst out laughing from astonishment. She slapped her hand over her mouth and sucked in her breath. She thought she could hear footsteps approaching very quietly. She had the feeling someone was listening, and that someone was not very far away.

"H-hello?" The word came out more like a whisper. She cleared her throat. "Hello!" This time, it echoed through the stairwell. "Is anybody there?" Her question lingered in the air. There was no answer. The silence made her nervous. From one minute to the next, goose bumps rose on her arms. Standing on tiptoe, she backed away from the hatch. Then at the stairs, she turned and stumbled down. Quick, keep going, don't stop... .

She had already crossed the hallway on the second floor when the piano started up again. With her foot on the top step, she paused and listened. The passage sounded much better now. *I helped do that,* she thought in amazement.

The light from the lobby below came up to meet her. She rubbed her arms to warm them up. Then she rushed down the last flight of stairs, through the lobby, and into the sunshine.

"Why don't you go outside for a while after dinner? It's such beautiful weather!" Birdie comes into the kitchen. Annoyed, I look up from my book, which is on the kitchen table in front of me, propped up against the fruit bowl. Since when is there anything wrong with reading? It's the only good thing about a boring summer vacation: lots of time to read. The best books are the ones you can crawl right into and forget everything else.

"All that sitting inside can't be good for you." She gets the bread and a couple of plates and starts making sandwiches. "It only makes it take longer before Robin is back."

"There's nothing to do outside. Everybody's on vacation." My legs are sticking to the seat of the kitchen chair. "And it's much too hot anyway."

I hunch over my book even further. I've just started the last chapter so I want to keep reading, even though I'm already sorry it'll be over soon.

When I have a really good book, I sometimes put off reading the end for a long time because I don't want to finish it. I'm afraid the story will just keep going on without me. And at the same time, I don't understand how I can miss something that really doesn't exist.

"I know what! Play one of those nice little tunes for your grandma."

She puts a plate of sandwiches between us and sits down across from me.

I take a big bite so I don't have to answer her right away.

"... such a shame that you don't do that anymore." Birdie takes an apple from the fruit bowl and starts peeling it. There's a clatter from the mail slot in the front hall. I can't help myself— I've got to see what it is, even though I know very well that it's too early for mail from Robin. She's only been gone two days. The only thing on the mat is junk mail. I walk back to the kitchen, still a little disappointed.

"Aren't you taking lessons any more from that nice man who used to live below you? What's his name again" —Birdie slices the apple in quarters— "Mazeltov?"

I shake my head and pick up another sandwich.

"Your father would have thought it was such a shame if he knew you weren't—"

"Birdie! Leave me alone!" Angrily, I jump up and snatch my book from the table. I don't need to hear the rest. I stamp up the stairs to my room and slam the door behind me. Why won't she leave me alone? I kick the orange paint can as hard as I can and drop into the blue chair. I try to continue reading, but what Birdie said keeps reminding me of Malakoff.

It's already more than six months since he brought the letters from Sky. And in all that time, I haven't been to see him once... .

I slam my book shut, thoroughly annoyed. Why was it so important for Robin to go to the boat? Now that I'm finally able to start getting my mind off last year.

There's a knock at the door. Birdie comes in and puts a bowl of fruit on the armrest without saying a word. Pieces of apple, strawberries, grapes, bananas. One by one, I pick out the grapes. She stands there staring at me with her arms crossed.

"That's how I got my nickname." She jerks her chin toward the plate. "And it's all your fault."

I give her a puzzled look.

"Don't you remember?" A surprised smile breaks through. "Birdie! One of your first words ... and I don't even like birds." She chuckles.

"You always loved grapes. I used to clean them for you, one by one. You'd throw back your head like a little bird and I'd pop them into your mouth. I called you 'birdie' every time, and you ate them up without ever saying a thing." She wags her finger accusingly. "But one time, you saw me coming down the street and you started yelling 'Birdie! Birdie!' " She laughs quietly. "And it stuck." She picks up the empty plate.

"Robin latched onto it right away. 'Now you've got a bird's name, too, like it or not,' she said. And what could I do? I was completely outnumbered." She shrugs her shoulders helplessly and walks to the door.

"More paint?" She taps a paint can with her foot.

"Wall paint. For over the purple," I tell her, with my mind still on that name. It's weird that I'm the only one without a bird's name. Sky had come up with one, but once I was born nobody thought it suited me.

"Not a bad idea." She takes a good look around before walking out. I hear her slowly make her way up the stairs as I stare at the purple walls. How could I have lived with that color all these months? Even in the middle of summer, it's depressing.

I look at my room and study it carefully. Actually, it's no more cheerful here than it is upstairs. There are even a couple of unpacked moving boxes in the corner near the window. They're filled with lots of old stuff, and I don't know what to do it.

The only thing I'm completely satisfied with is the blue chair. I stroke the bare armrests. It's going to look great with the orange. Suddenly, I can hardly wait to paint over the purple.

Robin was right. It's time things changed. I throw down my book and run upstairs, two steps at a time.

"I decided to go outside anyway!" I grab my bag and open the front door.

"Be home before it gets dark!" are the last words I hear as the door shuts behind me.

Mouse breathed in the outside air with relief. The sun burned her skin and made the goose bumps disappear. The door of the bus was open. She stuck her head inside.

"Dantzig? You need any help?"

Something began rattling under the bus. Then out rolled Dantzig, lying on his back on a little board with wheels. He waved to her with an enormous pair of pliers.

"I think I can manage on my own now," he said with excitement. "Just a minute—got to tighten something." He rattled back out of sight. "Actually, there's not enough room here for two to work anyway." His words sounded muffled.

Mouse sighed with disappointment and shoved her hands into her pockets. Her fingertips played with the bits of paper. She pulled them out and stared at the words and parts of words written on them. Then she lay down flat on her belly so she could look under the bus.

"Do you ever want that paper back?" It took a while before she could see Dantzig in the shadows.

"Paper?" Dantzig was turning something with the pliers. He groaned with the effort.

"The paper you used to measure those—those points." Her fingers slid over the g that looked like a pair of glasses.

"The points? Oh, you mean those scraps of paper." It was quiet for a minute. "You can throw them away. I've got plenty more."

"More?" asked Mouse eagerly. "Where?"

"Oh, you know. Where they always are. In the tool chest."

Mouse scrambled to her feet. She lifted the hammers and other tools out of the chest. At the bottom, sticking up through all the screws and nails, was a handle. She pulled on it. The bottom lifted out, nails and all. Beneath it was another bottom that was covered with pieces of paper. They rustled softly when she ran her hand through them.

"How did you get all those little bits of paper?" She scooped up a handful and examined them up close. They were all scribbled on with the same handwriting.

"A lot of litter blew in here a while back. One day, there were all these scraps of paper lying around everywhere. It was a real mess."

Mouse listened attentively. She held her hand up over the chest and made it snow.

"I picked up as many as I could. They were soaked because the weather had been terrible. Rain, wind, hail. It was last summer, just after—" Dantzig stopped in mid-sentence.

Mouse grabbed another handful and waited.

"I said to myself: Paper, that's good stuff. You can always use paper. So I dried it out and saved it."

"Just after what?" asked Mouse. Stuck to the very bottom was a much larger piece. She tried to pry it loose.

Dantzig sighed. "All this fuss about a bunch of old paper ... I can't get anything done!" Then he began to pound on something, making a terrific racket. Mouse finally got hold of a corner of the paper. She carefully pulled it loose. It was yellowed, and the top and bottom edges were torn. It had been written in pencil.

king back, it's good we didn't call
One tap of a swan's wing can break a person's leg.
Blowing your stack like that can hurt someone more

Swan's wing ... the word made her think of the mosaic in the lobby. She put her hands in the tool chest and then threw the scraps of paper on the cloth beside the bus. There were more pieces in pencil, but most were written in blue pen, or black. She picked up a piece with red letters.

st harbor we
strong that the
caught in a wave l

She turned it over the read the other side.

been drizzling
I'll bring you with
ve it storm? I'm countin
faster than the time at sea?), a

The best idea was to start with the red pieces, since there weren't so many of them. She fished them out of the pile one by one and kept on searching till she was able to fit two together. She found a third piece that fit as well. She moved them around, puzzling patiently, until she could finally read one whole piece.

terrible weather for days. We kept being tossed up in the air
and then we'd drop back down, ship and all. Most of the
customers were less than thrilled. All they wanted was sun
and smooth waves, bunch of fair weather wimps. So we had

to anchor in the closest harbor we could find. I once heard
about places on the ocean where the current is so strong that
the waves are as big as a house. They can be sixty feet high.
If a ship gets caught in a wave like that, it gets picked up like
a feather and dragged along for miles, until

Maybe it was a travel story, from someone who had been all over the world and had stayed here once, too. Mouse looked up from the paper. She didn't understand why the words she read made her feel so good. *Almost ... safe,* she thought with surprise. Too bad it took so long to put the puzzle together.

Maybe the traveler had slept in her room ... her gaze crept up from her own window and paused at the balcony doors on the top floor. This time, the doors were shut. She kept staring, her brow furrowed. There was something about those doors that bothered her. It was just as if she had forgotten something. But what?

A breeze blew the delicious smells of food toward her from the hotel. What time was it anyway? Dantzig hadn't made any noise for quite some time. He was still lying at the same place under the bus, but he wasn't moving. Mouse chuckled. Probably fast asleep.

She bent over the scraps of paper again and started to move them around. The wind caught a couple of them and blew them out of place. She snatched them back, but the wind quickly scrambled them up again. She wasn't getting anywhere this way.

Tape! she suddenly remembered. *I have a roll of tape in my room.* She quickly scooped up the bits of paper and stuffed them back into her pants pockets, which soon began to bulge. As she lifted the tray with screws to return it to the chest, something in the back of her mind kept bothering her. It had to do with those balcony doors.

Her hands hung in the air over the chest.

Balcony doors?

Yesterday she had been in this very spot and had seen something moving near the *balcony* doors, but when she got upstairs the *window* was closed. There wasn't any balcony in that room. She suddenly remembered how difficult it had been to push the dusty window open. How could she have overlooked that yesterday?

Had she actually been mistaken about the room? She narrowed her eyes and studied the face of the building. No mistake was possible. There were only two balconies on the whole front of the hotel, one on the top floor and one on the second. The two floors in between had no balconies, only windows.

Two floors in between?

She counted up from her own room on the second floor. Third ... fourth ... fifth floor.

Because there were only three flights of stairs, she had thought the fourth floor was the highest. She just hadn't looked carefully enough. She had never been to the top floor.

"What's the matter with you? You look as if you've seen a ghost!"

Fermer was standing in the doorway to the waiting room. He began banging on a pan with a big spoon as hard as he could. Dantzig woke up with a snort and cursed as he hit his head against the underside of the bus.

"Come and get it!" Fermer hit the pan a few more times with all his might. "Dinner's ready!"

For the first time since the move, I'm standing on our old street. It's as if nothing has changed in all that time. The shop on the corner is still open at night, as usual. They sell the candies that Malakoff is crazy about. I go inside. The candies are still in exactly the same place on the rack.

The guy behind the counter is someone I don't know. But next to the cash register, there's still the same box of marked-down junk. My eye falls on a roll of tape. Suddenly, I remember the white bag at the bottom of the moving box.

Armed with the candies and the tape, I hurry down the old familiar sidewalk to Malakoff's house. I can hardly wait to see him sitting at the open window, bent over some music book.

The curtains on the first-floor windows are drawn shut. Am I at the wrong house? Confused, I take a step back and look around. I haven't made a mistake. The curtains of Malakoff's living room and bedroom are closed. Why isn't he sitting in his regular spot?

The curtains at one of the windows are slightly open. Cupping my hands against the windowpane, I try to gaze inside. But it's too dark to see anything.

"What's this all about? Spying on strangers?" A heavy hand comes down on my shoulder. I turn around, terrified, and look into the angry face of the upstairs neighbor.

"Oh, dearie, is it you?" As soon as she sees that it's me, her expression changes. "I hardly recognized you. My, haven't you grown! Did you finally come to see the old man? Oh, wouldn't he have liked that, though. He missed you so much. I could tell."

Have liked? My ears start to pound.

"He's in the hospital." She points behind her with her thumb and shakes her head. "In a bad way. He put on a brave face, of course. You know how he is." She crosses her arms on her chest. "But he couldn't fool me. I see right through that sort of thing."

"What's wrong with him?" I can finally get a word in edgewise. "Is he going to be all right?"

"We have to wait and see. Things like this take time. It's all that smoking, you know." She puts her hands on her hips and leans over toward me.

"But tell me, dearie, how's your mother doing? Poor thing. Is she still so ..." She looks at me and shakes her head sympathetically. "I understand, you know. It's not that. I would have broken down under a whole lot less."

In a state of panic, I stare at her mouth, which keeps opening and closing, opening and closing. I can hardly breathe. I've got to see Malakoff.

In the meantime, I nod at random—yes, no—slowly slipping to the side, between her and the window. When I'm far enough, I break into a run and stick up my hand without looking back. Fortunately, the hospital isn't very far. Even though it's hot, I run almost the whole way.

Downstairs in the reception area, it's cool. I go up to the receptionist, completely out of breath. My throat is parched. It takes a while before I'm able to say who I've come to see.

"Visiting hours just ended. You'll have to wait until tomorrow." The receptionist looks at me from behind the counter.

"But I have to see him!"

He raises his eyebrows slightly.

"He's my neighbor!" I give him an imploring look.

"Not family?"

"Well, he is a kind of uncle," I try. I still haven't caught my breath. A telephone starts ringing. It's so cool in here that suddenly I start to shiver. The receptionist speaks a few words into the receiver and then holds it against his chest.

"You'll really have to come back tomorrow. I'm sorry. Afternoon visiting hours start at two o'clock." Without losing sight of me, he brings the receiver back to his ear and starts talking again.

One of the elevator doors is open. I look from the door to the receptionist. He sees what I'm thinking and shakes his head as he talks. Deeply disappointed, I turn around. I feel his eyes pierce my back until the glass doors slide closed behind me.

"I really didn't know how to deal with all those courses." Fermer looked around fretfully. In the middle of the waiting room, he had pushed four small tables together to make one big one. It was covered with a white tablecloth that almost touched the floor.

"And then I thought: What if I bring out the soup and you feel like something sweet?" He gestured at the table, which was loaded with dishes and bowls. It was a jumble of smells, all clamoring for attention. "Or you want something savory when I arrive with a dessert? So I'm serving everything at the same time." With an exaggerated bow, he pulled back a chair for Mouse.

"It looks wonderful just the way it is." She sat down, keeping a hand in each pants pocket so none of the little papers could fall out. Dantzig crept onto the chair next to her. He slid his belly under the tablecloth, which he pulled up to his armpits, and sniffed the nearest dish. As Fermer lit the candles, he started slurping loudly.

So I was right when I was looking for the piano on the fourth floor, thought Mouse. The sound did come from higher up. Her legs swished restlessly under the table, back and forth. Fermer sat down across from her and looked at her expectantly. She had to try to think about food. She ladled something from a random bowl and poured it onto her plate. It was a kind of clear green soup. She picked up a piece of bread and dipped it in the soup. It tasted sweet and ... a little nutty. "Delicious!" Suddenly, she realized how hungry she was. She smiled at Fermer, who was still staring at her. Would the animals know anything about the fifth floor? She swallowed and took another bite. She couldn't think about that now!

Dantzig pulled two little bowls toward him and dumped the contents onto his plate. With his mouth full, he launched into a report of his latest progress on the bus. Mouse listened with only half an ear.

What's the point of having a floor with no stairs leading up to it? she said to herself as she tried to stifle an impatient sigh. *Don't think about that now!* She forced herself to listen to Dantzig, who was just saying the rings were loose and that he was seriously thinking about taking the whole block apart once more.

"When the bus is running again," she asked as Dantzig paused for a minute and looked around for another dish, "what are you actually planning to do?"

"Ha!" Dantzig jumped up. "Then ... then the sky's the limit!" He held his paws as far apart as he could to show how big everything was. "Coming and going, everywhere and nowhere in particular." He sank back dreamily and pulled the tablecloth up a bit higher. The candlelight gleamed in his eyes.

"First of all, fetching the hotel guests and bringing them back, of course. Now that it's starting to look as if Fermer really can cook, it could get busy around here again." He tossed a piece of bread in the air and caught it in his mouth.

Fermer grinned. He cut a big pie into pieces and pushed a piece across the tablecloth toward Mouse. It tasted sweet and sour at the same time. Like cherries, yet different, somehow. She took another bite and nodded enthusiastically at Fermer.

"If you guys really want business to pick up, then something will have to be done about those letters on the roof," she said with her mouth full. It was out before she knew it.

"You starting in on that again?" Dantzig said irritably, pulling the rest of the cherry pie toward himself.

"As long as ... it says what it says, you'll chase everybody away." Mouse wiggled uneasily back and forth on her chair. "Even if the food is good." She glanced quickly at Fermer.

"I've said the same thing to him a hundred times myself, but he doesn't want to hear it," said Fermer. Using a teaspoon, he carefully served himself something from every dish as if he were putting a palette together with spots of every color.

"Because I don't buy it. What difference does a couple of letters make?" Dantzig looked grimly from one to the other. "As if one letter more or a letter less can keep somebody away. And if I don't do it, you'll just do it yourself anyway!" He angrily brushed aside a blob of pie. It left a dark red spot on the white tablecloth.

"All those wires mixed up together ... I can't make head nor tail out of it." Fermer shook his head ruefully and leaned toward Mouse. "It would be easy for him," he said confidentially. "If he could just stand on the roof, he'd have it done in no time."

"Oh, is *that* it! You're afraid of *heights*!" Mouse said with sympathy. "You don't have to be embarrassed about that. I am, too!" She shut her mouth with surprise. Was she really afraid of heights?

"I am not!" Dantzig jumped up with such force that it made the glasses tinkle. He snatched what was left of the cherry pie and stamped out, slamming the door behind him. But the door didn't latch very well, and it flew right open again.

Mouse was stunned. She looked over at Fermer, who didn't

seem bothered at all by the outburst. He placidly sniffed his plate, each time staring intently into the distance. After a while, he sighed and rubbed one paw over his belly with satisfaction. Then he put down the plate and stood up.

"This seems like a good moment for a little something extra," he said cheerfully, and walked briskly toward the kitchen.

Outside the heat drops over me like a clammy blanket. An ambulance zooms past. All sorts of thoughts are racing through my head. A car horn honks right behind me; I jump aside just in time.

Why haven't I been to visit Malakoff in all this time?

Because you were afraid he would see right through you, whines the voice in my head. *Because you were afraid he would guess your secret.*

Maybe he's been sick for a long time. The neighbor lady told me how much it bothered him that I never came by. What if it's too late? What if I can't patch things up with him anymore? Just like—

I walk as fast as I can to keep one step ahead of my thoughts. From the hospital through the old neighborhood to our new street, up the stairs, down the hall, down the stairs to my room, into the blue chair.

How will I ever make it till two o'clock tomorrow? Impatiently, I play with the bag on my lap. Through the fabric, I can feel the sack of candies ... and something else. The tape! Suddenly, I remember what I was going to do. I walk to the boxes near the window and pick up the one on top. Inside are old clothes, nothing else. The second box is full of forgotten toys. I unpack them all, one by one, but I don't find what I'm looking for.

My old stuffed animals are at the bottom of the box. I take them out and line them up next to the box. The last one is the rat. When he's out, the box is empty. None of the boxes contains my old white bag with the letters in it. Puzzled, I sit down in the blue chair with the rat still in my arms.

"I was sure I had put the bag in the box with the stuffed animals," I say out loud. I look at the rat on my lap. "Do you know where it is?"

The rat stares back blankly. After all this time, he's more yellow than white, but his little eyes are still gleaming. I was five when I got him from Sky, and my arm was in a cast. At first, I was a little afraid of him because he was almost as big as I was. He had a strange kink in his tail, which Sky managed to make up a story about right away. To take my mind off things, I try to remember it.

The story was about three rats whose tails were knotted together. When one rat wanted to go one way, there was always another one pulling in the opposite direction. So most of the time, they just sat there and let the other rats do all the walking for them. Everyone felt sorry for the rats so no one dared refuse them anything. They got more and more spoiled. Eventually, they came to be known as the Rat King.

Two of the three rats were quite satisfied with the situation, but the third rat dreamed of another life. He wanted freedom, so his tail had to come out of the knot. But as soon as he started fiddling with the tangle of tails, the other two rats began snarling at him. They weren't the least bit interested in being ordinary rats again because they'd have to give up their lazy life. And worse than that: They would have to give up their beautiful name. Finally, all the third rat had to do was look at the knot and the other rats would flash their teeth.

The rat decided he wouldn't give up his dream for all the tea in China, so he concocted a scheme. He started telling the other two rats a story that was so exciting that they had to listen, and so complicated that they had to pay attention all the time. It made them tired since they weren't used to doing very much. Because they were still curious and wanted to hear how the story would end, they struggled not to fall asleep. But the story got longer, and longer, and longer. The first rat dropped from exhaustion. And well before the knot was untied, the second rat was snoring away.

With his last drop of strength, the third rat untied the knot. Now that no one was resisting, it was as easy as pie. He tied the two other tails neatly together and put a big bow in the middle. Long before the two rats woke up, he was gone. He went into the wide world with a kink in his tail. The first person he ran into was me. With my arm in a cast.

Sky said he couldn't be called a Rat King anymore because that was the name of the three rats together. For a long time, I tried to think up another name for him, but I was never able to come up with a better one.

"I thought I heard you coming in." Birdie steps into my room. "I have an idea." She points from the paint can to the wall. "We don't have to wait. We can start tomorrow morning. What do you think?" She beams at me. "When Robin comes back, there will still be plenty to do. In the meantime, if you start looking for the brushes ..." She nods with satisfaction and leaves without waiting for an answer.

"Good idea," I say to the rat, and stand up. Oddly enough, thinking about that old story has calmed me down. I put the rat on the floor next to the paint can and follow Birdie out of the room.

Mouse peered around the door cautiously. Dantzig was sitting with his back against the wall and the plate on his lap, muttering. The evening sun was falling across the plain.

"Dantzig? Please come back inside. Fermer has been trying so hard."

She took a step toward him. "I shouldn't have brought it up! If I had only known you were so—" She didn't finish her sentence, afraid she would only make things worse.

Dantzig crammed the rest of the pie into his mouth and chewed silently.

"Maybe you're right. They are only letters, after all." Mouse sat down against the wall with a little space between them.

"No good rotten letters: *That's* what they are." Dantzig looked at the hill in the distance with a hurt look on his face. For several minutes, all that could be heard was the sound of him angrily smacking his lips.

"Time for a little something." Fermer came outside with a tray for them, which he laid on the sand. He had made an enormous tower of cream puffs. Mouse sat up with surprise. Fermer bent over, speared the top cream puff with a fork, and held it out to her.

"Those things give me no end of trouble. I'm about to pull them all down." Dantzig grabbed a cream puff from the left and the right side of the stack and gobbled them both up.

Mouse stuck the little fork into her mouth and stared at the tower. She forgot to chew. Suddenly, she understood why Dantzig didn't do anything about the letters. He couldn't reach them! He couldn't get to the fifth floor, of course. There weren't any stairs that went that far ... but there just might be an elevator! Mouse swallowed the wrong way and started to cough.

"All that business about words is pointless anyhow." Dantzig patted her absently on the back. "A great big fuss about ... about nothing. You can't touch them, can't sell them." With an angry gesture, he picked up three new cream puffs and crammed two into his mouth at once. "You can't eat them." He tossed the third one up high. It curved gracefully and landed in his open mouth.

"You can tell stories with them." Fermer waved his fork around as if he were writing in the air. He waited until Mouse had finished coughing before going any further.

"When the bus starts running again," he said as he pricked a cream puff on his fork and studied it closely, "I hope we get so many travelers that we fill all the hotel rooms."

He looked at them one at a time.

"When you have a lot of guests, there are bound to be a few who can make music." The fork danced through the air. "Or tell stories. Exciting stories full of adventures, about quests to faraway places into the past or the future. Just imagine. Every night. There won't be much waiting in the waiting room after that!" He grinned as if he could see it already. The red evening light was reflected in his eyes.

"And when everything is humming along nicely," he went on quietly, "I'm going to start a garden." Now his fork had become an enormous rake. "First the vegetable garden. That will be right up front. And a couple of trees for shade. Trees you can hang a hammock from. In the middle of a big field with flowers and herbs, everything all mixed up together." He dropped backward in the sand.

"And fruit. Every imaginable kind of fruit. Do you know how fantastic white pear blossoms show up against the blue sky?" He sighed and shut his eyes. Suddenly, the silence was broken by the sound of the piano. The tower of cream puffs was half gone. Dantzig, his eyes shut, muttered something under his breath. At exactly the same moment, Fermer started to yawn.

Wide awake, Mouse sat between them and listened.

The person who was playing must have used the dumbwaiter to get to the fifth floor. And if the pianist could do it, surely she could do it, too. All she had to do was figure out how to open the dumbwaiter hatch. She looked impatiently from Dantzig to Fermer. Were they asleep already? Suddenly, she understood what the buzzing was that she had heard in the hall. It was the sound of a dumbwaiter going up and down.

Dantzig smacked a couple of times and started snoring quietly. Fermer was still lying on his back. The music slowly became louder. Long rows of notes tumbled gracefully one after another into the open air.

As long as the pianist kept the fifth-floor hatch open, it was impossible to open the hatches on the other floors, of course. So the dumbwaiter couldn't move. And no one else could go to the top floor.

Dantzig began snoring more loudly. Every time he exhaled, his whiskers would tremble.

Mouse couldn't stand it any longer. Very carefully, so as not to wake the others, she stood up and looked up at the front of the building. The balcony doors on the fifth floor were open. Each time the neon lights went out, she thought she could see a weak little light shining behind the curtains.

She turned back for a moment. Fermer was breathing steadily. He was still grinning, even in his sleep. Dantzig had slouched forward and was snoring nonstop.

A plan was taking shape in her head. Standing on tiptoe, she stole past them and entered the hotel through the waiting room.

The more purple disappears under the orange, the lighter it gets in my room. My hands are all orange, front and back.

Time drags on. I glance over at the clock every other minute.

"Can't get much hotter than this." Birdie wipes the sweat from her brow and puts the roller in the empty can. "Maybe we'll get some thundershowers."

I keep working until there isn't a trace of purple to be seen. Only then do I straighten up. We stand side by side, viewing the results with satisfaction. Later, when the wall is dry, I shove the blue chair in front of it.

Finally, the clock points to one thirty. Birdie follows my glance.

"Want me to go with you?" she asks. I've told her about Malakoff. I shake my head. Walking with her to the hospital would take much too long.

"Get going then." She smiles. "I'll clean up."

I grab my bag from the chair and I'm already out of the room.

"And be sure to wash that paint off your hands!" she calls after me. I run up the stairs two steps at a time and shut the front door quietly behind me. Ten minutes before visiting hours begin, I'm standing in the reception area.

"You're too early," says the receptionist. It's the same one as yesterday. He winks and consults a list so he can tell me where I have to go. "Fourth floor. You can go right up." He points to the elevators on the other side of the entrance and waiting area. The doors glide open without a sound. I wait impatiently for them to close again.

The air on the fourth floor smells a little like a swimming pool mixed with soap. It's strange but not nasty. A male nurse comes up.

"Mr. Malakoff? He's down at the end of the hall," he says, and walks along with me. That "Mr." makes me laugh.

"He'll be so happy! He doesn't get many visitors." He laughs back.

"Is he going to be all right?" Now I'm not afraid to ask.

"Don't worry." The nurse puts a hand on my shoulder. "He just has to rest." He stands at the door and pushes me forward with a gentle prod.

There are two beds opposite each other in the room. One bed is empty. A strange man with his eyes closed is in the other. Just as I'm about to say it's the wrong room, the man opens his eyes and starts talking. My jaw almost drops. I recognize Malakoff from his hoarse voice.

"Hey, sweetie ... what a surprise!" Malakoff grabs a bar over his bed and pulls himself up. He looks weird in this bed, as if he were smaller than normal. His hair, which usually sticks out on all sides in a big bush, is plastered flat to his head. But he gives me a big smile. And from close up, I can see that his eyes are shining.

Behind his bed is a machine that keeps peeping. It has red numbers that light up. It's connected to a tube that hangs loosely over the edge of the bed. I hope it's not supposed to be connected to anything.

"Is it serious?" I blurt out nervously. My voice has a strange squeak to it.

"Not at all. I'm fit as a fiddle. False alarm!" He taps his chest where his heart is located. "They just want to keep me here a couple of days, for observation." He grins. "And now that I see you, I'm feeling better already." His eyes search my face.

"You weren't shocked, were you?"

"The neighbor lady said that you—"

"Has she been spreading wild rumors again? That woman should learn to keep her big trap shut!" He shakes his head, but he's still grinning. "It's so great to see you. You've grown!"

He's being so nice, it makes me shy. He doesn't say anything at all about neglecting him all this time.

"How's your new house?" He points to my hands. "The last time I saw you, you had lilac paint on your fingers. And now orange."

I tell him about my room. And about Robin, who's gone to the boat, and that Birdie is staying with me. Malakoff listens attentively and nods. When I don't have anything more to report, he leans back on his pillows.

"There's too much time in a place like this." He gestures around the room. "It's not good for a person to have so much time. I'm just sitting here spinning my wheels. You know what I miss? My music books ... but not with you here." He pats the blanket beside him.

"So your mother has gone to the boat?" He nods with approval. I cautiously climb onto the edge of the bed.

"What happened to Sky's stuff, anyway?" I ask out of the blue. I have second thoughts about the question before it's even out of my mouth. "I mean the stuff you picked up from the boat."

"You mother didn't want it. I gave it away to a horn player

who could use a few good instruments. All I kept for myself was the music Sky and I played together so much."

"Do you suppose ..." Suddenly, it sounds like a stupid question.

Malakoff raises his eyebrows inquiringly. I take a deep breath.

"The letters you gave me when you came back ... one was missing." I'm afraid to look him straight in the eye. "Do you suppose it ended up with his other things?"

A deep wrinkle forms in his forehead. After a while, he shakes his head.

"I didn't find anything else when I was cleaning up." He looks at me with his X-ray vision. "So that letter is important?"

I shrug my shoulders and try to look cool and indifferent. He stretches out his hand, the way he always does. I put my hand in his. With my eyes glued to my orange fingers, I suddenly blurt out everything at once. About the fact that Sky was supposed to come home for my birthday, but then he didn't come, and about my angry letter, and about that making it all my fault. And about not daring to tell Robin. And not daring to tell him, either, of course, which was why I hadn't come to visit, because he was sure to see straight through me and I couldn't let that happen. And sure enough, it was still true because it was happening right now, just like I said. And I keep rattling on and on.

He hands me a handkerchief with his free hand. Surprised, I take it. I just now realize there are tears running down my cheeks. I blow my nose and don't have anything else to say, but he's still holding my hand. I look up at him warily from the corner of my eye. Just when I think he's about to say something, a nurse comes in.

"You've got to get some rest," she says. The soles of her shoes peep with every step.

"My visitor and I still have something to discuss," says Malakoff. I look at him with astonishment. He sounds almost embarrassed.

"Then it would be better if she came back later. The next visiting hours start at six thirty." The nurse gives me a friendly nod but doesn't budge from the side of the bed. Malakoff looks at me helplessly. Despite everything, I have to laugh. I've never seen him like this before.

"You know what?" he says suddenly. "How about going to pick up a couple of music books for me?" His eyes lighten up. "If you bring them later, we'll continue our talk."

I nod in bewilderment and blow my nose one more time.

"Somewhere in this drawer is a key to my house." He looks at the nurse, who walks out of the room again, and points to the little cabinet next to his bed. "The one with the little boat on it."

There's only one key. It has a silver chain with a tiny little pendant. I have to look very closely to see that it's a boat.

"Bring a little Bach. I can never get enough of him. There's a stack on the kitchen table." He rubs his hands together with enthusiasm. "Always something new there to discover. Sky and I loved playing Bach together."

I nod. I've heard them often enough.

"Sky's books ... I haven't looked in them, not even once." He smiles a little sadly. "But every time I walk through the front hall, I think of him."

I laugh back, even though I don't quite understand what he means.

"I'm glad you told me all those things." He puts a hand

on my arm and squeezes it. "When you come back, I'll have thought about it." He squeezes me again.

"It's great you came to see me, sweetie. I feel like a new man."

A little embarrassed, I slip the key chain into my pants pocket. Suddenly, I think about the candies. I take them out of my bag and put them on his bed. He grins. "We'll save them for later." He puts his hand on them and leans back.

"There. And now I'm going to sleep. That nurse is right. You have no idea now tiring it is to spend the whole day in bed." He yawns and shuts his eyes with satisfaction.

Even before I get to the door, I can hear him quietly snoring.

When Mouse got to her room, she opened the balcony doors. The piano music wafted in. She began to recognize snatches of the tune, just as she had with the last piece. It sound as if it wouldn't be long before the pianist started looking for new sheet music. And to do that, he'd have to come downstairs. With the dumbwaiter.

She took her bag from the closet, pulled out the roll of tape, and placed the bag with the music books under her pillow. All she had to do was wait till it was quiet upstairs. And not fall asleep in the meantime.

She scooped out handfuls of paper scraps from her pants pockets and let them flutter down onto the bed. That ought to keep her awake, all right.

With her legs crossed, she sat among the scraps and started to sort them. Black pen with black, blue with blue, pencil with pencil. After a while, there were four little piles of paper. The smallest pile was the one with the red pieces. She had already figured out the one side of them this afternoon; it wasn't hard to fit them together again.

The piano passages became longer. Each time there was a pause, she waited with bated breath to see if the music would stop. But each time, the pianist continued playing.

She taped the tiny bits of paper together one by one. When

all the pieces were connected, she turned the whole thing over carefully.

you're not afraid of a good downpour, either, and I know you'd enjoy a storm like this as much as I do!) I was happy with your long letter. It cheers me up every time I read it. And I read it often, because it's been drizzling ever since we arrived here in the harbor at Rimini. Italy in the drizzling rain—what do you think? Someday I'll bring you with me, then the sun here will shine all by itself—or would you rather have it storm? I'm counting the days till I come home (how come the time there always goes faster than the time at sea?), and until

I hug you in my

It started to look more like a letter than a travel account. Too bad there were pieces missing from the top and bottom. Maybe Dantzig had used more pieces, or they had gotten lost. She took the yellowed piece of paper that she had loosened from the bottom this afternoon and stared at the penciled letters. *Swan's wing ...*

The music started to build and take shape. Quietly humming along, she scooped up the scraps that were written in pencil.

Was it the music that gave her such a good feeling or the words that were growing together bit by bit? Suddenly, she had a fierce attack of the yawns.

She had to stay awake! Blinking a couple of times, she opened her eyes as wide as she could and bent over the shredded paper.

of course, it's too bad that I had to leave sooner
planned. But you can't blame h
And I can say that, because you're
Looking back it's good we didn't call
One tap of a swan's wing can break a person's leg.
Blowing your stack like that can hurt someone more
than you yourself understand. So what I want to say is:
Think about it at least three or four times before you
      lash out.
Save your anger for me instead! After all, I'm the
      one who always
goes away. We're two hotheads who would be
      better off screaming
at each other every now and then. Angry or not,
      I was happy with
your letter. And as soon as I come back home, you can
      light into me
with that white wing of yours.

The lock opens with a dry click. At the halfway point, the door gets jammed on a pile of newspapers and envelopes in the entrance area. I quickly squeeze through the narrow space and stand with my back to the inside of the door, listening.

I can hear my heart pounding. Must be because it's so deathly quiet. Did it always smell so musty in here? I breathe deeply and take a couple of steps forward. The swinging door between the little entrance area and the hallway screeches so loudly that I let go of it out of sheer terror and almost run right back outside.

What am I afraid of, anyway? Malakoff himself asked me to do this! Yet it's weird to be in his house on my own. I take another deep breath and push the door open again, carefully now, so it only groans softly.

The hallway is nice and cool. The doors to the rooms are open, but they hardly let in any light. There's only a strip of light coming in from the kitchen. The door immediately to the right goes to the bedroom. The door to the living room is a little further on the left. I walk carefully around a table pushed up against the wall and peer in through the doorway. The curtains are shut. It smells like stale cigarettes in here.

"Hello?" I can't help saying it, even though I know very well that no one will hear me. My voice sounds hollow in the empty room. Without Malakoff, it seems much more spacious. The sun squeezes in through a narrow slit in the curtains. On the table in front of the window, there's an overflowing ashtray between the piles of music books. I see another one on the piano.

I walk on tiptoe past the old familiar cabinets in the back room that form a solid wall of sheet music from floor to ceiling. These cabinets have a lot more shelves than normal bookcases. The books lie flat in little stacks. The kitchen door is the only opening in the wall. I walk straight through the sheet music and into the kitchen. Yellow light streams in through the thin curtains. A tall stack of music books is on the table. The top book says *Bach*, just as Malakoff said it would. I hold open my bag and take as many books from the stack as my other hand can hold, sliding them quickly into the bag. Suddenly, I feel an urgent need to get out of here fast.

Passing through the swinging door, I hear voices outside. It's the shrill voice of the neighbor lady. I can tell right away. Very cautiously, I peer through the mail slot. She's standing directly in front of the door, talking to the man from across the street. Her words tumble over one another without a single pause.

After yesterday, I don't feel like bumping into her again. If she sees me leaving Malakoff's house, she'll want to know what I'm doing here, then she'll want to know how he is. And before you know it, she'll start in on Robin again.

So I'd rather wait till she's gone.

I quietly slip back through the swinging door into the hall. Clutching the bag, I pace back and forth, not knowing what to do. I peer around the door of the bedroom. That's a good place to wait. The window is right next to the front door, so I can hear as soon as the neighbor lady goes away.

With the curtain shut, it's as dark in here as it is in the

living room. It takes a few minutes before I can see anything. I drop gently onto the bed. There's a big stack of music books on the night table, and another one on the floor beside it.

I crawl into a corner of the bed and snuggle up with a few pillows that are leaning against the wall. All I have to do is wait until it's quiet outside—and make sure I don't fall asleep in the meantime.

But the babbling of the neighbor lady right next to my head ought to be enough to keep me awake.

How long had it been so quiet?

Mouse scrambled up, a piece of paper stuck to her cheek. She had fallen asleep with her head on the scraps of paper. Everything was all mixed up, except for the pieces she had taped together. She reached under the pillow and found the bag with the books. So it wasn't too late! She quickly swept all the scraps into the bag and put the bag in the closet. Then she put the key in her pants pocket.

It was quiet in the hall. One tiny light was on. She slipped out the door and walked to the dumbwaiter in her bare feet. Every time the wooden floor creaked, she paused. Still not a sound to be heard. It was dark in the corner near the dumbwaiter. She groped for the handle and pulled on it. As usual, it didn't move. She quickly climbed up the stairs. The hatch on the third floor was also shut tight. She still had one more chance.

The fourth floor was pitch-dark. She shuffled along the wall inch by inch until she felt the handle. Then she pulled with all her might. It moved! Very slowly, the hatch moved up a bit. Light came out through a narrow chink. Mouse put her shoulder under the handle and pushed. The hatch groaned softly as if it was grudgingly giving way. The strip of light grew wider. As she peered into a small, rectangular compartment, her eyes blinked from the brightness. Would she fit?

Inside there was a light, and next to it a panel with five buttons. Each button had a number beside it: from 1 to 5. There was a button for the fifth floor! Nervously, she tried to climb in. If she crouched down and cocked her head a bit, she could just make it. She took a deep breath and pushed the button marked 5. Nothing happened. Maybe she had to shut the hatch first. She wrestled one arm free and pulled on the handle. The hatch closed easily from the inside. As soon as the hatch snapped shut, the light went out. She couldn't see her hand in front of her face. The dumbwaiter began to move with a sucking sound. She couldn't tell whether it was going up or down. It sure was taking a long time! ... After all, she didn't have that far to go, did she? Was the dumbwaiter still moving? She waited, her heart pounding. It felt like she was running out of air. What if the dumbwaiter stopped and she couldn't get out? What if she started shouting and no one could hear her? Just as she opened her mouth to scream, she felt a shock. The dumbwaiter had stopped. She shoved open the hatch and rolled out, gulping fresh air with relief.

She had expected that everything here would be very different, but this floor was just like all the others. The same hall, the same doors. One of them was open ... that had to be the door to the fifth-floor room directly above hers.

Very quietly, she shut the hatch and walked down the hall on tiptoe. The room was dark. When she got to the doorway, she stopped.

Directly across from her, next to the balcony doors, a piano gleamed silently in the light of the neon letters. The keys shone pink. Cautiously, she moved closer.

There was an open music book on the stand above the keys. She switched on the piano lamp. Next to it was a crumpled piece of paper.

On the floor right behind the piano was a narrow mattress with the bedding all rumpled up at the foot. The other piano book lay open on the pillow. Right beside it, there was a piece of crepe cake on a plate. The big bed at the far end of the room was neatly made and undisturbed.

She looked at the crumpled paper near the lamp. It was full of musical notations that appeared to have been hastily written down. Something was scribbled at the top in blue pen.

Canon a 2 per Tonos, or The Stair Climber's Song
If you can't play it, don't you fret—
just whistle the tune before you forget,
like the lighthouse man (who's whistling it yet!)

The Stair Climber's Song ... Mouse frowned. Where had she seen that word before? Filled with curiosity, she slid onto the piano bench and placed the sheet with the music in front of her. It was a melody you could play with one hand.

With her right hand, she struck the first couple of notes, so softly that she herself could hardly hear it. The notation was swarming with sharps and flats, and she had to do her best to find the right keys. Finally, she managed to recognize it: It was the tune she had heard over and over again when she first arrived. After eight measures, the melody resumed, but this time one key higher. Strange. It sounded so simple, but it was so hard to play. Her fingers slowly climbed higher over the piano keys; she simply couldn't stop. She had long given up playing quietly.

"Where did you put them?"

Mouse shot up and quickly turned off the lamp. Her knee banged hard against the piano. Someone was casually leaning against the doorpost. How had he gotten here? She sucked in her breath and stared at the figure. All she could see was a silhouette, illuminated by the light from the dumbwaiter. An enormous shadow fell into the room. The dumbwaiter! She hadn't thought to leave the hatch open.

"The other books, I mean. Where are they?" The voice sounded harsh and angry. The shadow pulled itself away from the door and slowly came closer. Now that he was closer, he didn't seem so big. The pink light from outside kept shining on a face. On, off. It appeared and disappeared. It was the face of a girl.

Was *that* the pianist? Mouse fell back onto the piano bench in astonishment.

Was this the person the animals never wanted to talk about? The person they pretended didn't exist? A girl like herself, but half a head shorter? Her fears evaporated completely.

"You mean *my* piano books, the ones you took without asking?"

Mouse stood up. Each time the pink light flashed, she could see the girl a little better. She had the same wiry red hair as Mouse and the same dark eyes. But the girl's eyes were much angrier. *A reflection ... that isn't my reflection,* Mouse thought with surprise.

"I'm just borrowing them for a little while. I won't lose them. Really." The girl picked up the paper that had fallen from the piano stand. She pressed the sheet of music protectively against her chest and tried to smooth it out.

"What's your name?" she asked bluntly.

"Mouse," said Mouse.

"What kind of a name is that?" The girl laughed scornfully. "Even a mouse deserves a better name than that."

Mouse looked at her, flabbergasted. "In my family, everybody has a bird's name, except me." She listened to her own words in total amazement.

"How come you're hanging around with those animals downstairs?" The girl lifted the piano book from the stand and shut the lid with a sharp tap.

"The animals are nice, that's all," said Mouse. *Nicer than you,* she said to herself. "I don't see what you have against them."

"What I have against them?" The girl looked at her defiantly. "It's their stupid blabbering, for one thing."

"So you'd rather sit up here all by yourself?" Mouse stared back at her, finding this hard to believe.

The girl put her hands on her hips. "Would you like to spend all your time stuck with two talking animals, without knowing why and with nowhere to go?" She turned around abruptly and picked up the piano book that was lying on the bed.

Mouse looked at her sharply. *That's just what has happened to me,* she thought in astonishment.

"Use the dumbwaiter to send up the new books." The girl shoved the two books into Mouse's hands with such force that Mouse had to take a step back to keep from falling over. "You don't have to come yourself."

Mouse had just about had it with this girl. She seemed to be doing her very best to make people not like her. *If that's what she wants—fine with me,* thought Mouse.

Without saying another word, she walked into the hall and squeezed herself back into the dumbwaiter.

"Go live it up with those creatures of yours." The girl was following her. "They even carry your bag around for you, don't they?"

"I had lost that bag." Mouse reached out with her hand to push the button marked 2, but the girl grabbed her wrist.

"When I came here and I lost my bag, no one found it for me. And I ended up searching every nook and cranny."

"Then maybe you should have asked more nicely." Mouse pulled her hand loose and pushed the button. "Fermer gave my bag back to me. Dantzig had found it."

"Oh, please! Now they have *names!*" sneered the girl. She stretched the last word out as far as she could.

"What's your name, anyway?" snarled Mouse, who had started to lose patience. Instead of answering her, the girl grabbed hold of the handle.

"Make sure you send the dumbwaiter right back!" She closed the hatch with a loud slam. The light went out. The dumbwaiter started moving with a sigh.

"Right away, you hear me?" Mouse could still hear her shouting, but she was much too angry to be afraid. *Go jump in a lake,* she thought. You're not getting even one more book from me.

When she reached the second floor, she climbed out of the dumbwaiter and walked straight into her room and then to the closet. She put the two books in with the others. "Not a single one!" she said out loud. Then she threw the bag on the bed and flopped down next to it. *No wonder the animals didn't want to have anything to do with her,* she said to herself indignantly. *I'd be glad not to see her anymore myself.*

She stared stubbornly at the ceiling and tried not to pay any attention to the questions that were swirling through her head. How could the things that had happened to her also have happened to this girl? And was it a coincidence that they looked so much alike?

She sat up, fuming. She really didn't want to look like some angry girl who was sitting upstairs all by herself and who said mean things. And she really didn't want to think about it anymore, either. She snatched the bag from the bed and strode out to the dumbwaiter. Without even looking, she pulled out a book and threw it in. She hesitated a moment, then tossed the rest of the books in after it. At least, that creep wouldn't have to come to her room anymore. Before she could change her mind, she sent the dumbwaiter back up.

Slamming the door behind her, she went back to her bed. Up on the fifth floor, the piano began playing haltingly. She turned on her side and clicked off the light. But even in the dark, she could still see the girl before her, the wrinkled piece of handwritten music pressed to her chest. *The Stair Climber's Song ...*

She shot bolt upright. Suddenly, she remembered where she had seen that word before! She put the light back on, pulled the bag toward her, and turned it over. Her fingers searched through the pile of papers until she found the right one. It was written in blue ink. There were lots of them. Resolutely, she bent over the scraps and set to work.

for your letter! It was waiting for me like a bright light in the fog (which has settled in here and won't go away). All that smooth water and fog make me want to yawn my head off all the time. And once I've started yawning, I can't stop. So I walked to the pier to distract myself this afternoon. At the end of the pier, a lighthouse suddenly loomed up. The upper half was in the clouds. The door was ajar, but no one was inside. I felt like walking around with my head in the clouds, too, so I started to climb. The stairs turned and turned, around and around. I kept on climbing to the beat of a tune in my head, and only after a while did I realize that I was humming the Stair Climber's Song. Remember, the one I was going to play for you when I got home? It made me think about how beautifully you played for us, so I soon found myself with my head in the clouds even before I had climbed very far. As I thought about you, I made a circle along the upper balustrade, to the tune of the Stair Climber's Song. Their invisible world. Did you know you're a very good dancer? (And that dancing is a great way to keep from yawning?)

Our dance was interrupted by the lighthouse man, who suddenly popped up right behind me. I couldn't understand him, but he made it clear to me with gestures that I had to go back. Fortunately, he gave me a friendly laugh at the same time. On my way down, I was apparently still humming, because after a while I heard the lighthouse man softly whistling along, again and again and again, as if he couldn't stop, either!

Back on the boat, I looked up the piece right away and copied it out. Only the melody; I'm sure the old fiddler knows the other part by heart. I'll go ahead and send it to you. If you hold on to it for me, I'll know it will be there the next time I come home.

Actually it's a round, and it really has another name, but I think Stair Climber's Song is better. After every eight measures, the melody starts up again. And each time, it climbs one key higher. You can see it clearly on paper. But when you listen, it happens in such a sneaky way that you don't even realize it at first. Only after a while, do your ears start to notice.

Bach played jokes like this all the time. He liked to hide all kinds of puzzles in the pieces he composed. At the top of the music for this round, he wrote the word ricercar, *which means something like "search." So actually you're playing a kind of "I spy" with someone from hundreds of years ago, right through time!*

The more often you listen to his music, the more you discover. And the more you find, the more curious you get. And the more curious you get, the harder you search ... yes, I know, I'm babbling. I'll stop, don't worry!

If you're in the mood, write me general delivery in Helsinki (if you're fast), otherwise in Stockholm. I hug you in my heart.

P.S. That lighthouse man won't be able to get that tune out of his head, of course, because that's the way it is with random tunes. If a tune like that comes along, it's hard to get rid of it. And every time he whistles it, someone else will take it over, without thinking about it, because that's the way it is with a tune you just pick up along the way. So pretty soon, they'll be whistling the Stair Climber's Song all over the place around here!

"You can stop pretending she doesn't exist." Mouse burst into the waiting room. Fermer was crouching down at the outside door, turning something with a screwdriver.

"I've been to the fifth floor." She looked at him, waiting for a reply.

The door was wide open, and the morning sun came shining in. Its bright light made her dizzy. She had hardly slept a wink, trying to make sense out of all that shredded paper.

"Finally, the door shuts nice and tight." Fermer slowly straightened himself up. He gave her a friendly slap on the shoulder and walked to the bar. Mouse was right on his heels.

"I *told* Dantzig it wouldn't be long" —he shoved a plate of sandwiches toward her—"before you bumped into her, I mean."

"No wonder Dantzig mixed the two of us up." Mouse climbed onto a bar stool. She could hear Dantzig tinkering on the bus outside.

"It certainly is striking how much you resemble each other, at first glance. But when you take a closer look, you can see the differences." Fermer cocked his head and grinned the way he always did.

"Dantzig didn't want me to tell you about her." Fermer nodded toward the outside door. "He was so upset, that I was stupid enough to give him my word."

"But why?" Mouse took a sandwich from the plate. Fermer frowned at the plate and began turning it around absentmindedly.

"It must have been a year ago when she came here. I remember it as if it were yesterday," he said after a while. Mouse took a bite of her sandwich and waited impatiently for him to continue.

"It was one of those days when the weather takes a sudden turn. This terrible storm burst out of nowhere. As if winter had suddenly arrived, in the middle of the summer. It was so cold that I had to turn on the heat." He looked at her with wide eyes, astonished all over again by the storm.

"Suddenly, the door flew open and there she was. Dripping and shivering. A little waterlogged bird." His eyes slid past her toward the doorway. Mouse forgot to eat. Even outside, it had grown still.

"Heat on in the middle of summer! That had never happened before!" He looked from one heater to the other. "And since then, it's only happened one other time."

"And that other time ..." Mouse looked at him questioningly.

"Was the day you came." Fermer nodded. "As soon as I saw you standing there, I thought: This has already happened to me before, in exactly the same way. First the sudden storm, the cold, the heaters, and then ... exactly the same girl on the stoop. Dripping wet." Fermer gazed at her, deep in thought. "It was as if the time in between had vanished." He seemed to be staring straight through her.

"Before I knew what I was doing, I saw myself walk up to you. Just like the last time with her. It was all so automatic. I pulled back the same chair and I heard myself say exactly the same words." He frowned. "Almost ... as if I were being prompted to say it."

Mouse did her best to follow him.

"If everything was exactly the same as it was then, how did you know that I ... was different?" she asked.

"Because you responded differently." Fermer let go of the dish and leaned on the bar. "You weren't angry at all when I started talking to you. More a tad shy than angry." He smiled at the memory. "You just sat down on the chair I offered you."

"Angry?" Mouse thought back to that first afternoon. She had been frightened more than anything else.

"*She* was furious." Fermer jerked his head toward the ceiling. "From the minute I opened my mouth. She didn't want to sit down and she didn't want to talk to us. She just stood there with her arms crossed. She was so ..." He couldn't find the right word. Mouse thought about last night and nodded sympathetically. She knew just what he meant.

"She kept asking whether there wasn't someone she could talk to. So strange. *We* were there, weren't we? It was as if she thought we didn't count. She called us—what was the word again..."

"Childish."

Mouse looked around. Dantzig was standing behind her in the doorway.

"She thought we were childish. Because we talked." His eyes looked darkly from Mouse to Fermer. "Do *you* get it? I mean, *she* talked, didn't she?" He sniffed contemptuously.

"She didn't want to have anything to do with us. Right from the start. She acted as if we didn't exist. She began searching the hotel on her own. We were right behind her, of course, but she just waved us aside." Dantzig came closer.

"In the beginning, she did her best to get away from here.

Every morning, she'd take off again. But she was never able to cross the plain by herself." He grinned, but there was something a little spiteful about it.

"Every evening, she came back, angrier than when she left and she disappeared upstairs without saying a word. Back then, she was still in the room you have now." He crawled onto the stool next to Mouse.

"First we thought, she'll come around." Fermer took over. He picked up a sandwich and tossed it over to Dantzig, who caught it with one paw. "She'll come downstairs, we said to each other. But instead, she withdrew even further." He stared regretfully into the distance.

"She moved to the fifth floor as soon as she discovered the dumbwaiter, and we hardly ever saw her again. Since then, we try to stay out of one another's way. She only comes down when she needs something. Usually, I don't notice she's been in the kitchen till after she's gone."

Mouse turned to Dantzig. "Why is she mostly interested in you?"

Dantzig tore a sandwich in half with his teeth without saying anything and began to chew loudly. Suddenly, he jumped up, grabbed another sandwich, and ran outside.

Mouse looked at Fermer, wondering what was going on. He leaned on the tap and glanced at the door with a look of pity. From outside came the sound of hammer on metal.

"When she finally realized that she was never going to be able to cross the plain, she began to bombard Dantzig with questions about the bus. She followed him everywhere, making him a nervous wreck. He did his best, but he just couldn't get the thing to work." He shook his head to the beat of the hammer, which was keeping up a fast tempo.

"Then the teasing started. And Dantzig ... he takes every-thing so seriously. Even though I've told him a thousand times not to. If I didn't know any better, I'd almost think they like get-ting into each other's hair." He smiled faintly, but the worried expression came back right away.

"One day, it was as if Dantzig just gave up. Instead of tin-kering on the bus, he spent the whole day at the bar. And one thing soon led to another ..." His voice faded away. He was silent for a few minutes. "Dantzig hanging around all the time right under my nose, and then that girl up in the attic never wanting to do anything. All that inactivity made me *so* unhappy. It was like a contagious disease." A deep frown formed in his forehead.

"Things got messier and messier around here. At first, it really bothered me, but I just wasn't able to do anything about it. After a while, all we could do was ... wait. Wait until some-thing happened. But nothing ever happened. It was as if time had stood still. And we were time's prisoners." Fermer shivered. For a long time, he just stared ahead with a dull look in his eyes. Mouse didn't dare disturb him.

"Until the day you came." He looked at her searchingly. "As soon as you came through the door and sat down on a chair, everything was different. In fact, everything went back to normal. As if time had suddenly let us escape with a sigh." Fermer looked as if he himself didn't entirely understand what he was saying.

"Since then, everything's started to move. It's as if you had given time a little shove." He gestured around him.

"I'm remembering how to cook again. Dantzig is tinkering on his bus ..." Fermer pointed outside.

"Once he was sure you were someone else, Dantzig made me promise that I wouldn't tell you about the girl. He wanted to keep you two from meeting each other as long as possible. He was scared to death that she would win you over and that he'd have the two of you to contend with. But actually ..." He looked at her pensively.

"Actually, it's just the opposite. Even upstairs, things have begun to change." He pointed to the ceiling. "We're glad that now she can ... borrow ... your books." He winked. Mouse began to understand that Fermer saw more than she had thought.

"Until then, she just played the same endless song, over and over." He rolled his eyes. "Enough to drive you crazy. All we could do was pretend we didn't hear it."

"Now I understand why Dantzig got so angry about the letters on the roof," Mouse said suddenly.

"She won't let him in." Fermer couldn't help breaking out in a broad grin. "He thinks it's terrible that you keep talking about it!"

Mouse chuckled in spite of herself. But her laughter froze in her throat when a loud bang came thundering through the air, followed immediately by a low rumble. The noise came from outside. And above it all, they heard Dantzig screaming.

Fermer was the first to get to the door. Mouse rushed anxiously behind him. The second bang was so loud she could feel it. It sounded as if the bus had blown up.

I shoot up like a rocket. My ears are ringing.

What was that crash? I hold my breath and listen. Is that footsteps I hear? Are they coming closer? It's dark and stuffy all around me. It takes a while before I realize where I am. Then I realize what the crash was that woke me: It was the door slamming, right beside me on the front porch. Relieved, I hear the neighbor lady slowly walk up the stairs. Her footsteps recede into the distance. Then it's quiet.

I slip out of bed, grab my bag, and run out of the room. Get me out of here! And then, before I even know what's happened, I'm lying flat on my face in the hallway.

"I don't believe it ..." Fermer's voice rose no higher than a husky whisper.

Mouse was afraid to look.

"He did it ..."

Warily, she peered out over his shoulder. In the midst of a thick cloud of smoke stood the bus, shaking and trembling. Dantzig was behind the steering wheel, one paw hanging nonchalantly out the window.

"Everything changes here when you least expect it," muttered Fermer. He looked so flabbergasted that Mouse burst out laughing with relief.

"All aboard!" Dantzig slapped the side of the bus impatiently with his paw. "We're making a test run!" He tried to sound lighthearted, but his eyes were gleaming.

"You go ahead." Fermer gave Mouse a shove. "He'll like that. I've still got a few things in the oven."

Mouse put her foot on the running board. Suddenly, she couldn't resist the urge to look up at the hotel. Her eyes searched for the balcony doors on the top floor. Did she see something moving up there?

"Ready?" Dantzig pumped the gas pedal a few times. The engine roared. They shot forward even before the door to the bus had completely closed. Mouse fell onto a seat on the right side of the aisle. With two hands, she clutched the back of the seat in front of her. Everything quivered and thumped. From the corner of her eye, she could still see Fermer, standing with his legs wide apart, watching them. She had wanted to wave to him, but she didn't dare let go, even with one hand.

The red plain was full of pits and bumps. Whenever the bus shot up in the air, Dantzig shrieked with pleasure. Mouse joined in, laughing wildly. With each bounce, she'd fly up and hang suspended in nothingness for a few seconds before slamming back into her seat. Sometimes, her head almost touched the ceiling.

"Listen!" Dantzig raised one paw. The bus was weaving back and forth. "You hear that engine? What a sound ... the most beautiful music in the world!" Deeply satisfied, he growled along to the roar of the engine. As soon as he put his other paw back on the steering wheel, the swaying eased. His driving style made her very dizzy.

"The whole world is at your feet!" Dantzig cried. "Where do you want to go?"

Mouse grabbed the backrest in front of her and slid to the very edge of her seat. Outside there was nothing but sand as far as the eye could see, and who knows how much further.

"To the edge of the plain!" she shouted back. It had to stop somewhere. She leaned forward and gazed intently at the horizon.

"Then we've got to get going." Dantzig grinned and stepped on the gas. They shot forward with such force that Mouse toppled over backward onto her seat. Just then, there was a loud bang. Dantzig raised his eyebrows, lightened up on the gas, and shifted gears. Another bang.

"I've got to check that out," he muttered as he slammed on the brake. She lurched forward just as suddenly as she had been catapulted back, bumping her head against the backrest in front of her. Dantzig was outside before the bus had even come to a complete stop. By the time Mouse stepped off the running board, he was already mumbling under the hood.

She rubbed the sore spot on her forehead and looked around impatiently. They'd never get anywhere this way. The engine ticked quietly. Other than that, there was total silence. Or ... did she hear something? A faint sound, somewhere in the distance. She took a couple of steps. It came and went with each gust of wind. A kind of blare. And then a regular sort of drone. Like something keeping time.

"Do you hear that?" Mouse nudged Dantzig, who had just slid out from under the hood. "It sounds like music ... I think it's coming from over there." She pointed behind her. "We've got to go that way!"

Dantzig scratched his head and stood on the running board. "We've got to go back," he said, pointing in the opposite direction. "I'm worried about that banging."

"But just listen!" Mouse pulled on his arm and put a finger to her lips.

"I can't hear anything." Dantzig looked absently in the direction she was pointing to and shrugged his shoulders. Mouse pricked up her ears, but now she couldn't hear anything, either.

"If we keep on going, we could drive the whole thing into the ground." Dantzig slid behind the steering wheel and started the engine. He made a semicircle with the bus and stopped right in front of Mouse. Reluctantly, she climbed in. She kneeled backward on the seat and gazed through the rear window at the horizon. All she saw was sand. Had she just imagined that music?

"It could very easily be the ignition," Dantzig muttered after the next bang. Mouse turned around and dropped onto her seat.

"Or that rusty camshaft ..." He stared ahead with a worried expression on his face. Mouse shut her eyes and leaned back. The banging died down. But where did that rattling come from all of a sudden? She sighed and opened her eyes again.

It seemed to come from the seat in front of her. Something blue was sticking out between the backrest and the seat. It must have been shaken loose with all that crazy driving. She bent forward and tried to push it back in place, but instead it fell right out. She picked it up. It was a piece of paper.

Dantzig had tried to stop the rattling by folding the paper up at least ten times and jamming it between the seat and the backrest. Mouse smiled. He thought almost anything could be fixed with paper. She unfolded it.

It was a light blue envelope with AIRMAIL in blue printed letters in the upper left-hand corner. There was a tear where it had caught on a screw while she was pulling it. Wondering what was inside, she took a look, but it was empty. She could hardly make out the address. Apparently, the ink had gotten wet, which made the letters run.

"How did you get this?" Mouse leaned forward and waved the envelope.

Dantzig looked around. The bus swerved. She felt a wave of nausea.

"Just found it. Yesterday, I think," he said indifferently. "Or was it day before yesterday? Must have blown in with the storm, just like you." He winked at her, but his expression immediately turned serious with the sound of two bangs, one right after the other.

"Maybe it's the gearbox." He shifted gears and listened attentively. All that followed was a little pop.

"Was there anything in it?" Mouse asked eagerly.

"What do I care about that old garbage?" Dantzig exclaimed with sudden impatience. "I've got more important things to think about! What if the valves are leaking?" He stepped on the gas and threw his paws in the air in desperation. The bus swerved dangerously. The bang that followed was deafening.

Mouse quickly stuffed the envelope into her pants pocket. This was not a good time to bother Dantzig. She sat up straight and looked out through the front window. That was always the best way to deal with car sickness. She focused on the hill, which slowly got bigger. It took a while before she noticed that she was humming a tune. The Stair Climber's Song. *That's the way it is with a tune you just happen to hear along the way ...* she had read something like that in the letter she had taped together last night. She hadn't gone to sleep until she had taped together all the scraps written with blue pen.

Since reading that letter, she had been haunted by one particular question. How did the girl get hold of a piece of music paper with the same song on it as the one mentioned in the letter? Mouse remembered how the girl had clasped the paper to her chest and carefully smoothed it out.

She shrugged. Probably she had just found it somewhere, the way Dantzig had found the shredded paper. She tried to dismiss the question, staring stubbornly into the distance until the hotel finally loomed into view.

Fermer was climbing a tall ladder propped against the building in front of the waiting room. He was dragging an enormous piece of cloth behind him. Halfway up, he made a wobbly turn toward the bus and gave a cautious wave. Then he climbed further and started fastening the cloth onto the wall like a kind of awning. It was white with wide yellow stripes, which stood out cheerfully against the white of the wall. Fermer almost disappeared under it.

No sooner had the bus come to a halt than Dantzig was under the hood. Mouse cautiously came down the steps and leaned against the door, feeling very dizzy. *Maybe I ought to lie down for a few minutes,* she said to herself. She walked slowly into the lobby and up the stairs. First an almost sleepless night, then this ride ... no wonder her legs were shaky.

Deep in thought, she opened the door to her room and stopped dead in her tracks. There was a head of red, tangled hair on her pillow. Two spindly shoulders stuck out of the sheet. *Just like a bird,* thought Mouse.

She frowned, put her hands on her hips, and waited.

The girl turned slowly onto her back.

"I've been waiting for you all morning," she said. Taking her time, she stretched and folded her arms behind her head. Mouse watched with surprise as a broad smile spread across the girl's face.

"I was almost afraid you weren't coming back."

Thoroughly dazed, I scramble to my feet. My bag has flown from my hands. I grope along the wall until my fingers finally come upon the light switch. I've stumbled over the tall table next to the living room door. The music books that were stacked on the table are now scattered down the length of the hallway. I prop my bag impatiently against the wall. This is going to take a while. With a sigh, I drop to the floor and start gathering the books together.

"What are you doing here?" Mouse crossed her arms on her chest and scowled down at the girl. "I've given you all the music books I have. There aren't any more."

The girl kicked off the sheet and stuck her legs straight up in the air. There was a hole in the sole of one of her sneakers.

"You know what's weird?" she said, wiggling her feet.

Mouse shrugged her shoulders grudgingly.

"This." The girl jerked her head toward something white lying next to her. Mouse picked it up. It was a bag made of the same fabric as hers, with the same kind of strap. This one wasn't bright white anymore, though. It was dirty and worn to shreds. She turned it over and over in amazement. It felt familiar, as if it belonged to her.

"How did you get this?" she asked suspiciously.

"I had it with me when I came here. Just like you." The girl bent her legs and folded her arms around them. She looked over at Mouse and smiled.

Was this the same girl as the one she met last night? Mouse wondered in confusion.

The girl rolled over onto her side and pulled herself halfway up. "Do you think we look alike?" She propped herself on her elbow and gave Mouse a penetrating glance.

"A little," Mouse said curtly. Without looking at her, she put back the bag. She hesitated, still feeling irritated, but her curiosity got the better of her.

"How old were you when you came here?" she asked.

"Ten." The girl just kept staring.

"And now?"

"Still ten, of course."

"When do you turn eleven?"

"Eleven?" The girl raised her eyebrows. "Why should I turn eleven? I think ten is a nice number."

At least, that's one difference between her and me, thought Mouse, *because I'm almost twelve. Twelve?* She stared at the girl. I remember something else, she almost wanted to say, but she kept it to herself.

"Do you remember anything from before you came here?" she asked instead.

"*Before* coming here?" The eyebrows rose even higher. "I don't know if I was anywhere before coming here. I don't even know ..." She shot an uncertain glance at Mouse and then looked away. "I don't even know what my name is."

"I didn't know mine, either!" Mouse dropped down on the edge of the bed. She looked so surprised that the girl began to giggle.

"It's almost as if the same thing happened twice by accident." She pushed herself up further and moved over next to Mouse.

"How can that be?" Mouse gave her a sideways glance. The girl shrugged and began swaying her legs from side to side. Both of them fell silent.

"You know what Fermer said?" Mouse frowned. "He said it's as if time had stood still here. And that now it's started up again."

"If he means the place was dead before you came, then he's sure got that right." The girl jumped to her feet. "Since you've been here, things have finally started happening. You coming?"

"Where?" Mouse asked distractedly. If she could just sit quietly and think things out, it would all start making more sense.

"Upstairs, of course." At the door, the girl turned around. "I've been waiting all morning!" She hung her bag diagonally across her chest and motioned impatiently.

"By the way," Mouse said as she stood up. "What was in your bag when you got here?" She did her best to make it sound unimportant.

The girl shrugged. "When I found it after the storm, all that was in it was this." She pulled out the crumpled sheet of music paper with the Stair Climber's Song on it and waved it around a few times. "You first." She pushed Mouse toward the dumbwaiter. Mouse climbed in, but her mind was elsewhere.

"Send it right back, okay?" The girl pushed the button marked 5 and slammed the hatch shut. The light went out.

So the girl had the Stair Climber's Song with her when she got here.

I'll go ahead and send it to you, it said in the letter. *So you can hold on to it for me.*

If the Stair Climber's Song belonged to the girl, the letters would have to be hers, too. Or the scraps of letters, rather.

The dumbwaiter started moving.

They had fallen out of her bag when the girl had lost it, of course. Dantzig had found them as they blew across the plain— just like her music books, one year later.

Mouse stared into the darkness and tried to understand why

someone would tear up her own letters. *If I had received such beautiful letters, at least I'd take better care of them,* she thought. She felt a little jealous.

Even before the dumbwaiter had reached the top floor, she heard impatient pounding on the hatch from below. Mouse sent it back and walked to the girl's room. It was stuffy in there. The music books lay scattered all over the mattress.

She walked to the window and opened the balcony doors. The edge of the new awning fluttered cheerfully back and forth below her. Dantzig was standing on the chest and bending over the engine.

Shredded or not, if the letters belong to the girl I'll have to give them back, Mouse thought reluctantly.

Out in the hall, the dumbwaiter hatch opened. The girl hurried up to her and pulled her over to the piano.

"You have to help me." She pushed her onto the piano bench and slid in beside her. "There are some parts that I just don't get." She opened the book on the music stand and jabbed the notes with her finger. "This, for example. These measures. Would you show me how to play them?"

Mouse looked at the music and shook her head. "That's too hard for me. I ... I don't think I've played the piano for a long time."

"But, yesterday, near the dumbwaiter, I heard you whistle the music!" Her fingers drummed impatiently on the top of the piano.

"That's because I recognized the melody." Mouse hesitated. "I think I've heard it somewhere before."

"What were you doing with all those books then?" The girl's dark eyes were almost reproachful.

"I don't know why they were in my bag." Mouse looked

away. "I really can't play the piano very well. Not nearly as well as you."

"Really?" The girl's eyes began to glisten. "It's going lots better now, thanks to your books. Before that, I couldn't get any further than this one song." She laid a hand on her bag. "There wasn't a scrap of music in this whole stupid hotel." She leafed through the book feverishly and put her hands on the piano keys. The first measures went all right, but then her fingers started to stumble. After trying a bit longer, she slapped the keys impatiently with the palms of both hands.

"Play it again?" asked Mouse.

The girl started again. And whenever she got stuck, Mouse hummed a bit further. With her eyes on the notes, the girl played what Mouse sang. Now it sounded better. The more the girl played, the more Mouse began to remember. Now she sang along with the piano, then the piano played along with her. Slowly but surely, the melody began to take shape. It wasn't long before the girl could play it quite well on her own. Her fingers shot tirelessly back and forth across the keys.

Outside the engine started up once again. Mouse walked to the window and watched as the bus slowly made a circle in front of the hotel. Without any explosions!

She smiled. The bus tooted, the engine roared, and Dantzig shot away in a cloud of dust. He had long disappeared beyond the horizon when the piano finally fell silent.

"That was beautiful." Mouse turned around. The girl put her hands in her lap and stared at them, as if she were trying to understand how she had done it. Suddenly, she stood up, ran through the room, and dropped onto the mattress.

"Once I've learned all these pieces ... I'm going out into the world!" She pulled a couple of the music books closer and started stroking them. "I want to go everywhere, especially with other musicians. To all the places in the world where there are pianos ..." She spread out her arms with a book in each hand and sighed as if she could hardly wait.

Mouse sat down next to her.

"Why are you always so angry?" she asked out of the blue.

The girl shrugged and stared uneasily at her feet.

"It wears me out, too, you know." She looked over at Mouse. "Each time I promise myself never to do it again, but before I know it I'm furious—just like that—and then it's too late." She shrugged helplessly.

Mouse nodded. She knew just what the girl meant. Sometimes she lost her temper all of a sudden, but with her it didn't last long.

"Maybe ..." The girl hesitated. "Say the fox is right. About time standing still. Maybe that's why I stay angry."

They looked at each other and burst out laughing at exactly the same time.

"Now you don't look angry at all anymore," said Mouse.

"You see?" The girl grinned. "Now that time has started up again, it's all over and done with."

Mouse laughed with her. She began to like the girl more and more.

"Maybe I can think of a name for you, too," she said suddenly.

The girl looked at her with surprise, but then she shook her head. "I don't want any old made-up name." She stood up and walked over to the piano. "If it's not my own name ... then I'd rather not." She started picking out the Stair Climber's Song. She had set the sheet of music on the stand, but she didn't look up at it, not even once.

If she already has a name, thought Mouse, *then it should be here somewhere. If only I can find it...* She walked to the window, deep in thought. In the distance, she saw the bus rushing back in an enormous cloud of dust. *Good thing I'm not in there,* she said to herself with relief when she saw how wildly it was swaying.

"Why don't you come downstairs with me later on?" Mouse strolled over to the piano. "The animals aren't at all what you think. They really are nice."

The girl played on stiffly and said nothing.

"Fermer is really a great cook. And Dantzig fixed the bus!" Mouse sat down next to her. She heard the engine turn off. A door slammed. Someone yelled something.

The girl just played on. And when she got to the end, she started all over again. Mouse tried to follow the notes on the paper, but she kept losing track. It took a while before she realized that sound was coming in through the balcony doors. Was that... music? She looked at the girl. Did she hear it, too?

For half a second, the girl's hand paused. Then she kept on playing. Her cheeks slowly turned red. The music coming in from outside sounded different, but it went so well with the melody she was playing that it sounded like part of the same piece.

Mouse ran to the balcony and leaned over the railing. Beneath the window were two men. They were dressed in long coats, and both were wearing hats. They stood side by side, facing the building, both with open instrument cases at their feet. One blew on a clarinet. The silver keys glistened in the sun. The man beside him had a violin clamped under his chin. They took turns. The alternating tones wove effortlessly through the melody from the piano. Mouse held her breath. That was how it was supposed to sound!

She saw Fermer come out of the waiting room with Dantzig

right behind him. They stood there with their mouths hanging open, staring from the musicians up to the balcony and back again.

When the music stopped, the girl came to stand next to her. They both looked down. The travelers lowered their instruments. They looked up, took off their hats, and made exactly the same bow.

"Who are *they*?" The girl prodded her in the side with a pointed elbow.

"New guests!" said Mouse. "I thought I could hear them this morning, out on the plain. Dantzig must have bumped into them."

"What did I tell you!" The girl glanced at her. "Everything has been changing since you arrived." She turned around and ran down the hallway. "Me first!" she shouted. Soon Mouse heard the dumbwaiter start zooming into action. As she waited for it to return, she leaned against the balcony railing and calmly viewed the scene below. Slowly, one by one, more and more travelers got out of the bus. Some were clutching onto one another, others were leaning against the bus, their faces pale. Mouse chuckled. She knew exactly how they felt. Maybe she should explain to Dantzig that he ought to take it easy.

She watched as Fermer coaxed the travelers into the waiting room, each disappearing under the awning. Dantzig was busy dragging suitcases to the luggage storage area. Mouse wondered with a smile whether the hotel was big enough for so many guests.

Deeply satisfied, she let her gaze pass over the crowd far below until she heard the dumbwaiter come back. As she zoomed back down in the darkness, she could already hear the distant sound of the girl's cheerful voice rising up to greet her.

Crawling down the hallway on all fours, I finally get all the books gathered together. Then I stack them in a neat pile on the little table. Feeling relieved, I grab my bag and push open the swinging door. Right behind it there's one more book that had somehow slipped underneath.

As I pick up the book, I notice something sticking out from between the pages. I pull on it. Suddenly, I'm holding a light blue envelope in my hand. It says AIRMAIL, printed in big letters. An airmail letter. My eyes pass from the printed letters to the address.

My hands start trembling so much I can hardly read. But that doesn't matter. I've known my own name for a long time, as well as the handwriting that wrote it. I'd recognize that handwriting anywhere. It's one in a million.

"You want me to get in *there?*" With wide eyes, his violin case clutched to his chest, the musician watched as Mouse struggled out of the dumbwaiter in the kitchen.

"It'll never work. There's no way I can fit." He stared into the cramped compartment with a look of apprehension. He was quite a bit taller than Mouse, and it was a tight squeeze even for her. "And that goes for the other musicians, too, by the way. Are you sure there are no stairs going up that far?"

The girl nodded. "If you can't go upstairs, how are we supposed to play?" she asked with disappointment in her voice.

The musician lifted his hat and scratched his head. Then he strode through the waiting room and outside with the girl at his heels. Mouse had to do her best to keep up with them.

When they reached the door, a din of voices greeted them. Travelers were shouting instructions to one another and dragging around their instrument cases. Amid all the hubbub, one of the travelers knelt in the sand and opened his case. A few minutes later, the sound of an accordion could be heard. Someone else sang an unintelligible song to accompany it while a few others laughed heartily. Fermer was beneath the awning, lining up several small tables to make one big, long one.

"Mouse!" Dantzig was pushing a case that was bigger than he was. "You heard it right this morning!" He straightened himself up and pointed over this shoulder. "They were all drag-ging themselves around through the sand as if they—"

Suddenly, he spotted the girl. He looked from her to Mouse. Before she could say anything, he made a big loop around them and walked toward the waiting room, where he suspiciously observed the girl's movements from the doorway.

The girl ignored him. She rushed straight through the crowd and up to the violinist, who was standing right in front of the building and staring up at it thoughtfully. Mouse hesitated. She looked back at Dantzig once again and then followed the girl.

"I have a better idea." The violinist put down his instrument case resolutely. "If we can't go upstairs, the piano will have to come down to us." He made a gesture with both hands as if he were picking up something from a high shelf and setting it down in the sand. He had big hands that looked as if they were used to hard work.

"That thing weighs a ton," said Fermer, who came to stand next to him. "How are you going to get it down?"

"We can hoist it," Mouse shouted suddenly. "I've seen it done once before! It was with a rope. And there has to be a hook all the way at the top."

The violinist pushed his hat back a little and stared upward. "You're right. I believe there is a hoisting hook on the roof. And about that rope ..." He put his hands on his hips and turned to Dantzig, who was leaning in the doorway. "You got anything like that?"

Dantzig shrugged his shoulders sullenly and peered into the distance with a dark expression on his face.

"Maybe there's something in the workshop!" The girl jumped back and forth in front of the violinist.

"Ah. What an *honor*. She wants to *talk* to us!" Dantzig made an exaggerated bow in her direction. "We have to be careful, though. Before you know it we'll start acting—umm, what's it called ... ?" He pretended to be pondering something, his red eyes nailed to the girl.

Mouse held her breath.

"Oh, yes!" His voice broke. "Child ... ish." He pronounced it as if it were two separate words. Mouse looked apprehensively from him to the girl, who had already opened her mouth.

"Wait!" she cried before the girl could say anything. "I remember there was a truck, too, with a kind of crane. Couldn't we use your bus instead?" She ran to Dantzig, grabbed him by the arm, and looked at the bus. Everyone looked with her except Dantzig, who was still staring at the girl.

The violinist looked from Dantzig to the girl and then with raised eyebrows to Fermer, who shrugged with a sigh and rolled his eyes.

"That bus of yours ..." With his hands in his coat pockets, the violinist sauntered over to Dantzig. "Isn't that a nineteen fifty-two model?"

Dantzig nodded without taking his eyes off the girl.

The violinist whistled. "You don't see very many of them these days. It's quite an achievement that you've been able to keep it running."

A couple of the other musicians murmured in admiration. Dantzig had to do his best to maintain his grouchy stare.

"The power of that engine—it's enough to blow you away." The violinist gestured toward the bus with reverence. "Hoisting down a little old piano would be a cinch for a warhorse like this. But" —he threw up his hands— "it's not meant for such dinky little jobs, of course." He looked from the bus to Dantzig with sympathy.

"Well ..." Dantzig looked flattered. "That's all true. On the one hand." He smoothed out his whiskers undecidedly. "On the other hand ... it does have a good towing hook." His eyes shot from the violinist to the bus and back again. "And it would be a shame not to—"

"What a tremendous idea! If we can use the bus, we'll have it down in no time!" The violinist clapped him jovially on the shoulder. Dantzig looked around, slightly bewildered, as if it had all been decided a bit too quickly.

"Great! There's a good sturdy rope near the back door." Fermer motioned to the girl. "You and I will go upstairs and secure the piano." He disappeared around the corner with the girl right behind him.

Even before Mouse and the musicians had shoved all the suitcases aside, Dantzig was pulling the bus up to the hotel. Fermer soon appeared in the fifth-floor window and threw the rope over the hoisting hook. The violinist caught the far end. No sooner had he tied it onto the towing hook than the engine started rumbling and the bus shot forward. "STOP!" roared the violinist. He lifted his hat and wiped his brow. The bus came to a standstill with a shriek. The rope was completely taut.

More and more musicians gathered around the bus. "Back!" shouted someone. "No, man, forward a little first!"

Dantzig blithely waved aside all instructions. The bus crept forward, its engine grumbling. The piano was raised inch by inch until it balanced on the edge of the balcony. Fermer gave it a careful push. Suddenly, there it was, dangling in the air, gleaming in the sunlight, and hanging at a dangerous angle.

The motor roared, and the bus began to back up gradually. Slowly, the piano descended. The further it dropped, the more it began to sway back and forth, until it bumped against the wall at the third floor with a dull thud. Everyone held their breath in alarm. The bump immediately stopped the piano from swaying—but other than that—nothing happened.

Quietly rumbling, the bus crept further, and the piano slid down the wall little by little before landing in the sand with a quiet groan right in front of the lobby doors. Dantzig cut the engine. In the sudden stillness, everyone stared at the piano, speechless.

"We'll put it in the lobby," said Fermer, sticking his head out between the doors and opening them wide. "That's where the most room is, and it'll look very distinguished there."

A group of musicians helped push the piano through the sand toward the door. It creaked with every movement. But once it crossed the threshold, it rolled easily on its wheels up to the edge of the mosaic.

"It's perfect right here!" The girl looked enthusiastically from face to face. Finally, she looked at Dantzig, who had just come into the lobby. Before he knew what was happening, she ran up to him and threw her arms around his neck. Shocked, he tried to wriggle free, but she held him tight and kissed him on both cheeks. Everyone stood around, gently laughing. Mouse chuckled along with them.

"I have a lot to do," Dantzig muttered when the girl finally let him go. He smoothed out his whiskers as if nothing had happened, but his eyes were glistening. Mouse thought she could see him blushing beneath his white fur. The girl opened the cover of the piano and cautiously hit a few notes.

"Doesn't sound bad at all," said one musician, who was trying to get into the lobby with a case shaped like a gigantic violin. Dantzig held the door open for the man and then shot out past him.

More musicians were coming into the lobby and opening up their instrument cases. To keep from getting in the way, Mouse sat down on the lowest step and just watched. The girl walked comfortably among the guests and gazed with curiosity at all the instruments that were emerging.

Fermer crossed the lobby and said something to the girl. She nodded and shouted something back that Mouse didn't understand. *You can see she feels right at home here,* Mouse thought with surprise, just like Fermer. She watched him lift a tray over his head with an experienced twist and walk nimbly among the musicians. Dantzig came back into the lobby with a few tools clutched under one arm. He smiled at Mouse as he passed and slipped up the stairs, humming a tune. It was as if everyone here suddenly had something to do. *Everyone except me,* thought Mouse. She stood up, crossed the lobby, and slid out the door.

It was muggy outside. The sky had begun to cloud over. She strolled a short distance in the direction of the hill. The sounds from the piano and the other instruments came floating up behind her. Indecisively, she turned around and stuck her hands in her pockets. It was only when her fingers touched the paper that she remembered the envelope. She pulled it out carefully.

The ink was smeared so badly that the writing was almost indecipherable. All she could read of the name was the first letter. That was an *M*. Or was it a *W*? The address was practically washed away.

edge Road, she was just able to make out. She recognized the g that looked like a pair of glasses. The same handwriting as in the letters ... She studied the postage stamps closely. *Poste Italiane* was printed in black letters over bright orange flowers. If the envelope also belonged to the girl, the name on it would have to be hers. She held it a little closer to her eyes. An *M* or a *W*. That could be anything ...

"Looks like rain." Fermer had come out through the lobby doors and was peering into the sky, overcome with happiness. "That means it's time I started working on my garden!" He stacked up the empty glasses and hurried into the waiting room. Soon the tinkle of glass blended with snippets of music coming from the lobby.

Mouse put the envelope away with a sigh. *At least I have something else to give her,* she thought as she opened the door to the lobby.

"Mouse!" The girl came up to her, beaming. "The musicians say I can go with them when they leave! Dantzig has already promised to take us." She laid a hand on Mouse's arm confidentially and whispered, "Did you know he's really very nice?"

Mouse chuckled.

"And we'll come back here between trips," the girl rattled on. "But Fermer has asked us to stay for a little while right now. He says we're good for the clientele." She could barely conceal her pride. "He hopes our music will attract guests."

"I have something for you," said Mouse. "Something I found." She walked to the stairs and beckoned. The girl took a step backward and stopped. She looked around at the musicians, not able to make up her mind.

Mouse burst out laughing. "You just wait here. I'll be right back," she said, and ran up the stairs. When she got to her room, she took the bag out of the closet. *How could she not be happy with beautiful letters like these,* Mouse said to herself. She stroked the bag with one hand and felt a strong impulse to look inside just once more ... but then she shook her head. She had waited long enough.

She hung the bag over her shoulder and closed the closet door. One stray scrap fluttered to the floor. She picked it up and hurried outside.

"Give us an A from that piano of yours!" she heard from the lobby. Halfway down the stairs she stopped.

The girl was sitting at the piano in the middle of the crowd below, playing one note over and over again, always the same one. The musicians repeated the note, made some adjustments to their instruments here and there, and played it again. The A sounded different on every instrument. All the sounds clamored together restlessly as if they couldn't wait to get started.

Mouse shut her eyes so she could hear better. Her fingers played with the scrap of paper in her hand. The sounds began to blend more and more smoothly, until after a while she couldn't tell which instrument was playing what. It was a single sound that floated up through the lobby—a sound that hadn't been there at first. *It seemed as if … as if anything could happen,* she thought, suddenly very happy. She opened her eyes and looked at the scrap of paper.

give!
a hothead just like me
didn't call you Swan!

Swan … she couldn't get the word out of her mind. Her eyes went from the yellowed paper to the white bird in the mosaic below. *A swan is a bird,* she thought. But when it's written with a capital letter, it's a name, just like Mouse. She stared at the girl. *I've got a beautiful name in the back of my mind,* flew through her head suddenly. *Just the thing for a girl like you.*

Mouse ran down the stairs, through the hallway and over to the piano. She stood right behind the girl and leaned forward.

"Swan?" she whispered.

The girl stiffened. Slowly she turned around.

"That's my name," she said softly. Her dark eyes were one big question mark. She looked into Mouse's face. "How did you find it?"

Mouse grinned triumphantly and opened her mouth to tell her about the scrap. She knew exactly where it was supposed to go: with the yellowed piece of paper. What did it say again?

Suddenly, she closed her mouth. Something held her back.

"How did you know?" Swan asked insistently.

Mouse didn't answer. She stared in confusion at the wooden puzzle under her feet. There was something that didn't add up.

"Nobody's as good with names as Mouse is," Fermer said proudly. He walked up behind them and picked up a tray as he passed. "She found my name, too," he shouted over his shoulder from the door to the waiting room.

"I still don't get it ..." Swan shrugged her shoulders. "But who cares? The most important thing is that it fits!" She looked at Mouse and threw two arms around her neck. Mouse closed her eyes and smiled.

"Are we going to do this thing, or what?" The violinist tapped the piano with his bow and began to play. Swan let go of Mouse. She looked at her with a radiant smile, clapped her hands a couple of times, and turned to the piano, her attention focused on the music once more.

With snatches of ideas racing through her head, Mouse took to her heels. She had to go outside. She couldn't think in here.

At the door, she paused and looked once again at Swan, who had raised her hands and joined in at that very moment. She played along with the musicians effortlessly—as if she had never done anything else in her life.

There's no air in here. I can't catch my breath. I stuff the book, letter and all, into my bag and swing the front door open.

Is it warm outside? I just can't stop shivering. I close the door behind me, turn the key, and slip it into my pants pocket. Without thinking, I start to walk, automatically, criss-crossing through the streets. My thoughts twist and turn, just like the path I'm taking. A letter from Sky to me ... A letter I never received. Why not? And how did it end up in Malakoff's house?

Malakoff's words ricochet through my head. *Every time I walk through the hall, I think about him...* Now I understand what he meant. The music books on the table in the hall were Sky's books. *I haven't looked in them, not even once.*

Suddenly, the pieces start falling into place.

I never received the letter from Sky because he was never able to mail it.

My head starts feeling strangely light. At a crosswalk, I lean against the traffic light and watch the light on the other side of the street turn green, then red, then green again.

Malakoff picked up Sky's things. The letter must have ended up among the books when he was cleaning. And Malakoff never saw the letter because he never looked inside the books.

I bump into someone. Or into his suitcase, to be exact. I'm

standing in the middle of the lot at the bus station. The man turns to me and asks me something I don't understand. I open my mouth to reply, but all I can do is stand there with my teeth chattering.

The table under the awning was deserted. A little further on, Fermer had measured out a plot of ground with four stakes and was digging in the soil with a couple of musicians.

Mouse sat down at the corner of the table, as far as possible from the lobby. She put the bag on her knees and rummaged through it until she found what she was looking for: the yellowed paper with the missing corner. She put it on the table in front of her.

The scrap fit exactly.

give!
a hothead just like me

Looking back, it's a good thing we didn't call you Swan!
One tap of a swan's wing can break a person's leg.
Blowing your stack like that can hurt someone more

That was what didn't add up. Mouse stared at the letters until her eyes started watering. If the girl was called Swan, then these letters were *not* written to her. They were meant for someone who *wasn't* called Swan. Someone with another name ...

Mouse looked up.

A name that started with a *W* or an *M*. That could be anything ...

The talk and laughter coming from Fermer and the musicians wafted over her in snatches. A new piece of music had started up in the lobby.

The piece of paper blew onto the ground. She bent over to pick it up.

"Aren't you supposed to be a part of all this?"

Mouse shot bolt upright, caught completely unawares. On the other side of the table stood a musician with a friendly look on his face. She hadn't heard him coming.

"Part of all this?" She stuffed the piece of paper into her bag. "Doing what?"

He pointed to the lobby with his clarinet. In his other hand, he carried an instrument case.

"Making music." He sat on a chair across from her with his case on his knees and started taking his instrument apart.

"Making music is more Swan's thing," said Mouse. "I don't play the piano anymore. I used to, when I ... when I was her age." She listened to her own words with astonishment. *I'll just stay as old as I am now,* sprang into her head all of a sudden. *Ten's a nice number, I think.*

She stared absently at the parts of the clarinet, which were lined up in a row on the table between them. One, two, three, four, five pieces.

"Music is better with words," said Fermer. He walked up behind them, headed toward the workshop, and came back outside a few seconds later with an enormous rake.

"Words, eh?" The musician looked at her pensively. He picked up one of the parts of the clarinet, blew on the silver keys, and started rubbing them with a cloth.

Mouse nodded. Suddenly, she pulled the blue envelope out of her pocket and pushed it across the table to the musician.

"Can you tell what this says?" She pointed to the first letter. The musician bent over and frowned.

"*A, W* I'd say ... or maybe an *M.* I can't read the rest. By the way, that reminds me" —he pointed to the bus with the part of his instrument— "this afternoon, I saw something over there." Suddenly, his arm stopped, suspended in midair. From far away came a loud scream.

"Can somebody HELP me?!"

The musician stood up, walked under the awning and looked around. First left, then right.

"UP HEEEERE!"

The musician bent his head back and raised his eyebrows with a smile. Then Fermer came walking up. "What are you *doing* up there?" he shouted anxiously. Mouse came closer, wondering what was going on. High above them was Dantzig, standing in the gutter. He was holding on to the T. The letter was at least twice as big as he was. He was leaning forward at a dangerous angle and swaying with a pair of pliers in his paw.

"Can somebody turn on the light?" He pointed with the pliers to the letters left and right.

Fermer put down the rake and walked toward the workshop, shaking his head. The musician was still staring upward, and he absentmindedly began rubbing the silver clarinet keys on the front of his jacket. Back and forth, back and forth.

"Now you can see I'm not afraid of heights!" Dantzig performed a couple of dance steps from the T to the E and back again. His silhouette stood out against the dark sky. Suddenly, the light began to flicker. The H, the E, the L—just once—and the O, and the T a few seconds later. Mouse could hear the tubes hum.

HOTEL, it said. The letters flashed on calmly. And off. And on.

"Now there's nothing to keep them away!" Dantzig's triumphant cry filled the air. "The guests, I mean!" He waved one more time, jumped back through the hole in the O, and was gone.

"Somebody else who's good with words." Laughing, the musician looked from the letters on the roof to Mouse.

"What I wanted to say ... that envelope of yours makes me think of something."

He gestured for her to wait, strode to the bus, and hopped inside. Mouse sat down on the edge of the table and watched him with curiosity. He walked up and down the aisle for a few minutes, looking for something. Suddenly, he bent down. And when he straightened back up, he was holding something in the air.

"I saw this lying on the floor this afternoon while we were riding around." He came out and waved a piece of paper around. "It was folded up at least ten times. Frankly, I thought it was just a piece of trash, until I saw that envelope of yours." He held it out to her. "I don't know whether you can still read it. It's pretty battered. And the letters are so small ..." He shrugged. "Maybe you know what to make of it."

The paper was light blue, just as blue as the envelope.

Mouse took it carefully and stared at the wriggly letters. At the g's that looked like glasses. She could hardly breathe. Suddenly, she remembered who wrote those idiotic g's. She pressed the paper to her chest with one hand, her eyes searching around for a quiet spot.

"The weather's turning." Fermer picked up the rake and pointed upward. "Maybe we should take down the awning, before—" He looked closely at Mouse.

The bus, she thought. *It's quiet in there.* She stood up and took a few steps forward. From the lobby, she heard someone laughing. Swan ...

Mouse paused. She turned around and looked hesitantly at the door.

"You seem to have found exactly what you were looking for." Fermer set his rake against the wall and nodded at her, as if he were answering a question she hadn't asked. Not out loud.

She turned back toward the bus.

"Don't forget your bag." Fermer held it up. Mouse took the bag from him as if she were sleepwalking. Fermer grinned his grin once again. Then he turned around, pointed to the awning, and said something to the musician.

Snatches of music came wafting from the lobby. Mouse listened as Swan's voice wound its way through the melody.

A drop fell on her hand. The wind pulled her hair. Another drop. Suddenly, there were goose bumps on her arms. Wobbling a little, the paper still held against her chest, she walked in the direction of the bus.

I can't stop shivering. I'm walking right alongside the buses that have just pulled up. I can still feel the warmth of their engines. People pass me on every side, the way they usually do, as if nothing was going on. I zigzag between them to my bench and sit down, my back against the wooden hut. The crowd around me calms me down. I breathe in the smell of gasoline and put my bag on my knees, like a little table.

I take out the envelope and examine it closely. The postage stamp hasn't been canceled. Just what I thought. Sky wrote the letter and put a stamp on the envelope, and before he could mail it ...

Instead of opening it, I spend a few minutes staring at that stamp. It's as if the orange of the flowers has rubbed off on my fingers.

Using Malakoff's key, I slice open the envelope along the upper edge. There's a thin sheet of blue airmail paper inside and a sheet of white. I take out the white sheet. It's crowded with Sky's scrawly handwriting. My hands are shaking so much that it takes a while before I'm able to read the first words.

You could already smell the rain.

I can feel a smile spread across my face. I recognize the sentence immediately. It's the beginning of the story Sky wrote for me, the story I had stuffed in with the angry letter I'd written him, without even thinking about it. Sky had simply sent it back!

Now I know for certain that he did receive my letter. His answer must be in the envelope. The shivering gets worse. Read the letter, stupid! What are you waiting for?

My fingers feel paralyzed. I just sit there like a block of wood, staring at the envelope. The squiggly handwriting jumps back and forth before my eyes, as if it were just as nervous as I am.

Two women walk past, deep in conversation. The click of their heels keeps time with the rhythm of the words pounding through my head. *If you don't show up for my birthday, you're the ROTTENEST father I know ... Just stay there and good riddance!*

An answer has been waiting for me all this time, without my knowing it. Right nearby. And now that I've found it, I don't dare read it. Not yet. I'm afraid of everything that might be in the letter.

I pick up the envelope and put it back in my bag. Stalling for time, I put the white paper on my knees and bend over it.

It's quickly getting darker. I have to squint to read the scrawly letters. A strand of hair blows in my face. I push it impatiently behind my ear, but it's just a little too short and keeps coming loose. The voices of the travelers fade into the distance, along with their hurried footsteps. The humming engines fall silent. The bus station disappears. I forget everything around me. My eyes begin to water from the strain of staring. I shut them and take a deep breath. I can already smell the rain.

The smell of the gasoline calmed her down. Mouse sat on the running board, out of the wind. With her bag on her knees serving as a little table, she tried to smooth out the sheet of blue paper as best she could. The paper seemed to have gotten wet at some point, and it turned bumpy when it dried. Here and there, the letters were no longer legible.

It was quickly growing dark all around her. Another drop fell. Mouse looked toward the hill, which appeared and disappeared in the blinking pink light.

She took a long, deep breath of fresh air and bent over the paper.

Dear Mouse,

I was happy to get your letter, even though smoke was still rising from it when I tore it open.

You know how lucky it was that I got it at all? If we had left this morning according to plan (the engine is working!), I would have missed it. But, apparently, a storm is coming, so we decided to stay in the harbor one more day. Kind of overdoing it if you ask me. At least I haven't noticed any bad weather. But I'm glad for the delay just this once because it gave me a chance to go to the post office, where your letter had just arrived.

Of course, you have every right to be furious with me. No reason is good enough not to be with you on your birthday. If only I could grab time by the scruff of the neck and give it a twist. Then I'd travel backward in time, back to you, to be with you well before your birthday just to be on the safe side. But I can't do anything about it now.

I can understand why you're angry with me. But why did you get so angry at the animals in the story? So angry that you didn't want to have anything to do with the story anymore and didn't even want to work on it? If it were up to you, I'd never find out what happens next—or what happens to that girl, and that's almost more than I can bear!

Don't you secretly feel a little sorry for her? There she is: in a deserted hotel, out in the middle of nowhere, waiting to see if anything is ever going to happen. What's to become of her?

Nothing! Absolutely nothing is to become of her. She's a prisoner, caught in a beginning that has no end. She and the animals, who've been trapped in an endless afternoon nap at the bar. Forgotten by time. A girl like that has lots of plans, of course, but none of them will amount to anything at this rate.

So if you don't want to do it for me (understandable) or for the animals (what's so bad about talking animals anyway?), do it for her! Don't you realize that only you can rescue her from her nightmare? Her fate is in your hands. It's your story. I only came up with a beginning.

That's why I'm sending it back. Do whatever you want to with it. Change anything you don't like. Tear it into a thousand pieces and start all over again. Or throw it away if you really have to. It's up to you to decide what becomes of it. I can't do that for you.

Dear angry daughter of mine, I hug you in my heart. And I secretly hope, without your knowing it, that a sequel to the story does appear sometime in the future.

Starting tomorrow, the distance between me and the two of you will get smaller every day, even though it's slow going. I'm sending you two great big kisses, one for each cheek. Anything else would be too heavy for an airmail letter.

Sky

P.S. Give your mother a really big hug for me as soon as you've cooled off. That's an order! No, even bigger ... that's right! That'll have to be good enough for now.

"Don't you have to go home?"

Someone puts a hand on my shoulder. I look absentmindedly at the bag on my knees. There's a friendly face to go with the voice. It leans over me and smiles. Raindrops spatter on the peak of his cap. Behind him is a big bus, chugging and shaking. Dark spots appear on the sidewalk at my feet. The smell of gasoline mixes with the smell of wet stones.

"You were already sitting here when I started my route this afternoon. That's hours ago." The friendly face looks at me questioningly. Raindrops tap gently on my bare legs. My cheeks are wet. Surprised, I wipe them with my free hand. Is that rain, too?

"Don't you have a raincoat? You're going to get soaking wet." He looks up at the sky, his hands in the pockets of his uniform jacket.

"I don't have far to go." I fold the blue paper up carefully and put it in my bag. The rain is falling harder. The areas of light gray on the sidewalk are getting smaller and smaller.

"Wait a minute!" The driver walks to the bus and jumps inside, taking all the steps at once. The engine falls silent. The only sound that can still be heard is the tapping of the rain. When he reappears, he has an umbrella in his hand.

"It's already late! Won't they be worried about you at home?"

He sits down next to me and does his best to hold the umbrella over the two of us. It's raining so hard now that the little drops dance in the street. The rain splashes up against my bare ankles.

"I must have lost track of the time. I always do that when I'm reading a story." I put my hand on my bag, on the paper I've just tucked inside. What else is in there, anyway?

Only now do I remember Malakoff. The music books!

"I've got to go to the hospital!" I jump up with a start. "I'm not too late for visiting hours, am I?"

"If you hurry, you'll just make it." The driver stands up and looks at his watch.

I hang my bag around my neck, the strap running diagonally across my chest. For a bag with music books, it's not very heavy. I put my hands on it. They are music books, aren't they? I try to shift the strap so I can look inside.

"Everything all right?" The driver holds the umbrella a little higher and gives me a worried look. "You sure are shivering all of a sudden!"

I open my mouth, but my teeth are chattering so hard that I can't speak.

"You know what?" He taps on his watch a few times. "Get in. It's almost time for me to go, and the hospital is on my route."

It's warm in the bus. The rain is drumming on the roof. I sit down on the edge of the front seat, right behind the driver.

"Hold on tight!" he calls out. The engine starts chugging again, and we're off. I think he just said something, but it goes in one ear and out the other. Clutching my bag, I stare at the windshield wipers as they swish from left to right. Each time they reach the halfway point, one of them squeaks. The bus rocks me gently back and forth. The driver leans forward and peers intently at the road. He starts whistling a random tune.

"Where do you want to go?" he suddenly shouts. He makes a wide gesture with his arms and gives me a quick sideways glance. "The whole world is at your feet!"

I burst out laughing. "First to the hospital, and then around the world," I shout back. I'm feeling better already. The bus rides over a pothole, and for a second I'm suspended in midair. I push myself backward in my seat till I can feel the backrest. I love buses, especially when they go nice and fast. Too soon the illuminated letters of the hospital come looming up.

"Special stop for emergencies!" calls the driver. He pulls up right in front of the entrance. The door swings open even before the bus has come to a halt.

"You sure you're all right?" He lays his arm on the steering wheel and turns toward me. I nod and stand up, my bag hanging firmly from my neck. "Thanks for the lift."

He raises one hand as if he were signaling to stop and motions me out with the other. I jump out of the bus, over the puddles and onto the sidewalk. The rain has almost stopped.

The engine roars, and the bus goes right through an enormous puddle, splashing water everywhere. He honks. And then he honks again, extra long. A few people at the entrance turn to look.

I wave with two arms, even though I'm sure the driver can't see me anymore. Watching the bus pull away, I walk slowly backward toward the entrance. The doors slide open behind me with a sigh. I turn and enter the reception area. Suddenly, I'm in a big hurry to see Malakoff. I can't wait to tell him what I've found.

9 781608 980871